SOMETHING IN THE WATER

Sydney felt a tightening in her stomach as she looked at the pool, which was partially hidden by the greenery. The underwater lights were on, and she thought she saw something floating, something that looked very much like a woman's hair.

The pulse in her throat grew more rapid.

Sydney had to be careful as she walked along the curved pathway that led to the pool. Walking slowly also gave her a chance to come up with an alternate explanation for what she'd seen, or thought she'd seen.

Then she reached the wooden deck that surrounded the pool and saw that it hadn't been her imagination.

A woman's body floated facedown in the shallow water of the pool, her hair fanned out in a halo around her head. She wore only a white slip, slashed and tinged red with blood from several stab wounds in her back.

Even without seeing the woman's face, Sydney knew she'd found Martina Saxon . . .

PATRICIA WALLACE

BLOOD LIES

ZEBRA BOOKS
KENSINGTON PUBLISHING CORP.

For Andy

Other Sydney Bryant Mysteries

SMALL FAVORS
DEADLY GROUNDS

ZEBRA BOOKS

are published by

Kensington Publishing Corp.
475 Park Avenue South
New York, NY 10016

First printing: May, 1991

Printed in the United States of America

We love without reason, and without reason we hate.
Jean-Francois Regnard

Prologue

December

The flames reached at least thirty feet into the night sky, and even from where he stood in the middle of the street, Victor Griffith could feel the heat the fire gave off. He brought his camera up and verified what his instincts told him; as impressive as the fire appeared in real life, it was strictly ho-hum city through the viewfinder.

What he needed was something to give the photograph perspective, to show how intensely the fire raged. The old standby—a silhouette of trees against the flames—had been done so often that it embarrassed him to even consider it. Which he did, if only for a moment. Then he lowered the Pentax and frowned.

One of these days, if the gods were kind, he'd snag the shot he'd dreamt about since he was a cub reporter with a Kodak: by getting down on his belly and shooting upwards through the frame of a child's tricycle. The human interest would be enough to gag a giraffe.

But the gods weren't in a generous mood tonight. The house, windows boarded up and apparently abandoned, was situated on an otherwise barren lot.

If he believed in staging scenes, the way some of the broadcast media did, he'd toss a trike in the back of his van and be done with it —

Sirens pierced the night with a suddenness that brought his head around in time to see the first fire truck turn onto the street. He could see the driver's startled look a moment later as the truck swerved to a stop only inches from where he stood.

Firemen jumped from the truck like fleas deserting a dead dog. They trailed the canvas hose between the nearest hydrant and the front of the house.

Or what was left of it.

Standing on the running board, the driver shouted into a radio mike, struggling to make himself heard over the siren melody provided by a second fire truck, a police car, and an ambulance. Adding to the clamor was the hiss of water as it hit the flames and boiled into steam, and the cellophane crackle of burning wood.

There's nothing like a good fire, Victor thought, and wiped his eyes, which were tearing from the acrid smoke.

The cop came up beside him, a sour expression on his face. "What the hell are *you* doing here?"

"Gathering news." It was his standard reply, and it earned him an even sourer look from the cop, one of the old guard who believed the public's right to know was just so much liberal hippie hogwash. Victor flashed his Press card and grinned, pleased that he hadn't lost his touch as a tweaker of official nerves.

"You sure you didn't set it?"

"Set it?"

"That's what I asked. It wouldn't take but a match tossed in the right place."

"I won't dignify that with an answer. I am nothing if not pure of—" He flinched as a main support gave way in the house and portions of the roof caved in, releasing a shower of burning embers.

"You're pure, all right. Pure bullshit."

Victor drew himself up to his full six feet six inch height. "Well, I suppose if anyone would know bullshit when they saw it, you'd be the one."

"What do—"

Usually he savored any opportunity to exchange insults with authority figures, but he noticed a Volkswagen Rabbit pull to the curb just beyond the ambulance, and all at once he lost interest in anything else.

Martina Saxon got out of the VW and took what was left of his breath away.

"—interfering with a police officer in the performance of—"

"Hold that thought," Victor said abruptly, and took off at a trot down the street toward her. When he was half the way there, she looked in his direction and a smile lit up her face.

Radiance, he thought. The fire's glow seemed to fade in comparison.

9

"Victor," she said as he approached, and laughed from deep in her throat. "I should've known you'd beat me to it. Don't you ever sleep?"

He swallowed, hard. "Not much, actually. Did you hear the call over the scanner?"

"Saw the glow in the sky and followed it." She brushed a strand of silky blond hair out of her eyes. "To tell you the truth, I haven't quite mastered the scanner . . . the only thing I can decipher is an occasional 'Do you copy?' And I don't."

"You will." Was it his imagination or could he smell the light fragrance of her perfume?

"So what's the story here?"

Victor told her what little there was to tell, watching her instead of the fire, which seemed to be succumbing to the firemen's valiant efforts. "The bottom line," he concluded, "is that whoever started the fire probably did the city a favor."

Martina blinked. "A favor?"

"Now they won't have to pay to tear the house down when the neighbors start bitching that the place is attracting transients and druggies."

After a moment, she nodded. "I suppose you're right."

"Aren't I always?"

This time when she laughed, she put her hand on his arm. "Not a chance."

Victor tried to will her incredible sable brown eyes to remain looking up into his, but she glanced back toward the fire.

"Still," she said, "someone lived there once."

The wistfulness in her voice caught him off-guard, but before he could react, she was gone. Reporter's notebook and pencil in hand, she cornered the fire captain and was doing what any good journalism intern should do: get the story from a credible and quotable source.

Which was why *he* was here, he reminded himself. He was the professional, she the amateur, and by all rights, he should be the one getting the who-what-where-when-whys. If only she didn't look so captivating chewing on the eraser of her number two pencil while she listened to the fire captain talk. Try as he might, he couldn't raise one iota of professional jealousy . . . although if the captain moved any closer to her, he'd be tempted to turn the hose on the source and to hell with a quote . . .

Victor sighed. Everything had gotten more complicated since Martina Saxon walked into his life.

The time had come to do something about it.

Chapter One

Sydney waited until the third ring to answer the phone. "Bryant Investigations."

"I'm sorry," a woman said. "I must have the wrong number."

There was a click breaking the connection, and then a dial tone. Sydney dropped the receiver into its cradle and made a notation of the time—ten fifteen a.m.—on the legal pad she kept next to the phone.

It was the thirteenth wrong number this morning, all from the same caller. Last week there had been a total of a hundred and three wrong numbers. The week before, eighty-seven.

The calls were more of an annoyance than anything else. And although the detective in her was curious as to who she'd angered enough to evoke such a response, she thought it best to leave the matter to the phone company.

The customer representative who'd taken her

13

complaint had offered the option of having the number changed, but since it was her business number, she was reluctant to do so. The expense of changing the number on all of the stationery was not inconsiderable, but besides that, she didn't want to give the caller—whoever the woman was—the satisfaction of having gotten to her.

Instead, she'd agreed to keep a log of the dates and times of the calls. The phone company would, they said, handle it from there.

Personally, she wouldn't care to have those guys after her; even now, after the break-up, A.T. & T. was a force to be reckoned with.

Sydney drummed her fingers on the desk, waiting for the phone to ring again. When it didn't, she got up and went to the window to look out. She adjusted the venetian blinds, squinting at the sunlight, and only just managed to keep from jumping out of her skin when the office door opened behind her.

"Sydney, as I live and breathe."

She turned to see Victor Griffith filling her doorway, height-wise at least. Tall and gangly, he had, since she'd seen him last, traded his Prince Valiant hair-cut for a perm. With a head full of curls atop that skinny body, he resembled an overwrought Q-Tip.

"Like it?" he asked, evidently noticing that she'd noticed.

If you can't say something nice, her mother's voice advised. "Well. It certainly is a change."

Victor smirked. "Makes you want to run your fingers through it, doesn't it?"

If her fingers were holding barber's shears. She

shook her head, returned to the desk and sat down, then regarded him with more than a little suspicion. "What are you after this time?"

"After?"

"What do you want?" It was not an idle question; Victor was forever working an angle. What puzzled her was that her caseload was down to nothing at the moment—which was why she had time to keep track of wrong numbers—and she couldn't imagine what story he could possibly be hoping to weasel out of her . . .

Victor sat on a corner of the desk and gave her a wounded look. "I'm here," he said in a hushed tone, "to engage your services."

"My . . . what?"

"I want to hire you, Sydney. Or rather—"

Here it comes, she thought.

"—I want to call in that favor you owe me. I'd like you to conduct a discreet investigation into the background of a young lady of my acquaintance."

The favor in question had been incurred last June while she was investigating the murder of a seventeen-year-old girl at an exclusive private school in La Jolla. A secretary who Victor had unaccountably charmed tipped him off—after typing the warrant—that an arrest was imminent. He, in turn, had told Sydney.

So she owed him. And this, apparently, was payback. "Background check, huh?"

He nodded, his enthusiasm making his curls bounce. "It won't take long, a day or two tops." He made a show of looking around the office, at the

15

empty 'in' basket, the now-silent phone. "I can see how busy you are."

She refused to be baited. "And just what is it you want to know?"

"Oh, the usual." He waved a dismissive hand. "Is she involved with anyone. Does her lifestyle put her at risk. That kind of thing."

Alarms were going off in her head. "Victor . . ."

"If you can spare the time, I'd like to find out a little about her family history, too. I'd hate to find out there's an ax murderer in the family just when the blade's splitting my skull."

"Victor. You don't mean you want a Lover's Profile, do you?"

"I do, exactly." His pale-lashed hazel eyes stared intently into hers. "I'm in love, Sydney, for the first time in my life."

She leaned back in her chair, amazed. Although that did explain the perm.

"Don't look at me that way. I know you probably think I'm a cad—I haven't missed those smoldering glances you've thrown my way—but what we had between us was mere physical attraction."

Sydney nearly choked. "Smoldering glances?"

"But, well . . . you and I are not destined to be, and I'm counting on you to be a good sport."

"Seething glances, maybe."

"Whatever. Anyway, what I feel for Martina is different than what we had. This—" he covered his heart with his hand "—is real."

"I'm happy for you," she said. And although they'd had their run-ins over the years, she meant it.

"Thanks. But before I begin my pursuit of the

fair lady, I want to know that . . . that she hasn't
. . . that she doesn't . . . well, you know."

In fact she did know. AIDS had changed the
complexion of dating, and there were any number
of private investigators who were making a good
living off conducting the kind of background check
Victor wanted.

A Lover's Profile was designed to uncover all
manner of potentially deadly physical indiscre-
tions, as well as a few financial ones.

Sydney had never accepted a tell-and-kiss case,
nor did she care to now. But she didn't see any way
to get out of it — a favor was a favor, after all — and
so she pulled the legal pad in front of her, flipped to
a blank page, and sighed.

"What's her name?"

Victor made no attempt to hide his satisfaction.
"Martina Saxon."

"Middle name or initial?"

"I don't know."

"Date of birth?"

He shrugged. "That I don't know."

"Address?"

"I don't know." He grinned sheepishly. "I was
hoping you could find out."

"Phone number?" She could look up the address
in the reverse directory.

"I don't know."

"Victor." She rolled the pen between her thumb
and index finger. "Why don't we make it simple;
what *do* you know about her?"

"What do I know about her?"

Seeing the dreamy look return to his eyes, she

clarified: "Occupation, place of employment, that kind of thing."

"Well, she's a journalism student at SDSU, and an intern at the *Union*."

This summer, after five years working as a stringer for Associated Press, Victor had gone legit, taking a job as an investigative reporter for the *San Diego Union*. Blessed with an uncanny ability to smell a breaking story a mile away, he was a prize catch for the morning paper.

"Is that where you met her? At the paper?"

"A masterful deduction. If I were paying you, I'd have gotten my money's worth already."

"Don't push your luck." She wrote down 'SDSU' and 'Union.' "What else?"

"Else?"

"—do you know about her?"

"Let me think." He frowned, scratched his nose, looked up at the ceiling, closed his eyes, then shook his head. "Not a lot."

"How long have you known her?"

"Since July."

"Six months? And pretty much all you know is her name? You have spoken to her, haven't you? I mean, this isn't one of these worship-from-afar things, is it?"

"Of course I've spoken to her," he said, sounding indignant. "Just last night I ran into her at the scene of a fire—"

"How romantic."

"Oh, and that reminds me: she drives a VW Rabbit. Light blue convertible with a white top. Personalized plates with her name . . . Martina."

"I'm afraid that's not going to be much help." Her contact at the Department of Motor Vehicles could no longer run I.D.'s over the phone since that young Hollywood actress had been tracked down by a crazed fan and killed. As a licensed P.I., she could still get certain information from the DMV, but now all requests went through Sacramento and the process sometimes took weeks.

Knowing he seldom was without a camera, she asked, "Do you happen to have a photograph of her?"

Victor actually blushed. "No. I didn't want her to catch me taking her picture and have her think I was some lovesick puppy. Besides, that would be invading her privacy . . . she might not like that."

Sydney refrained from pointing out that he was asking her to violate that same privacy, in spades. "How about a description, then."

"She's blonde," he began, and his expression turned goofy in an instant.

The boy had it bad. Sydney wrote down an abbreviated and objective version of the description he gave: Blond hair, brown eyes, five foot six, slender build, age estimated to be twenty-two or thereabouts.

"Okay," she said when he finally ran out of steam. "Is there anything else you can think of?"

"No, not really."

"What's her schedule at work?"

"It varies. But she's usually in on Monday afternoons, so you can get started today."

"Hmm. Now, what about other co-workers? Is she close to anyone at the newspaper?"

"Not that I'm aware of, and I've been watching. She's cordial but not chummy, if you know what I mean. Not the type to socialize with the gang after work. Comes in, does her job, and goes home."

Sydney found it intriguing that Martina Saxon could spend six months among journalists — arguably the snoopiest people on earth — and seemingly not have cast a shadow.

"Well," she said, "I'll see what I can find out about your intended."

"Today?"

If enthusiasm really were contagious, Victor would be headed for quarantine. "All right," she said, "today."

Chapter Two

The phone rang again as Sydney was locking the office door, but she decided to ignore it. The answering service would pick up after the fifth or sixth ring, and if anything required her immediate attention, they'd page her. Otherwise it could wait.

As for her "wrong number" log, did it really matter if she missed a few calls? Not likely.

Besides, she'd spent so much time in the office lately, she was risking a serious outbreak of cabin fever. And she was, she realized, eager to be on a case, *any* case. The past few weeks of relative idleness had been an ordeal, a trial by monotony.

Although by now she should be used to it; it was this way every year. The holidays distracted people from their problems. Husbands still were cheating on their wives—and vice versa—but no one wanted to have their suspicions confirmed amid the relentless good cheer of the season. Employees helped themselves to unauthorized bonuses, workers exaggerated the extent of their job-related injuries, and deadbeats skipped out on their bills, but only those with the hardest hearts were looking to bust them for their bad deeds while Christmas carols filled the airwaves.

Come January and it would be a different story. Good will toward men seldom survived the cold, clear dawn of the new year.

In her business, January couldn't come soon enough.

Sydney drove to the Union-Tribune building on Camino de la Reina in Mission Valley. She made a left into the only entrance and coasted to a stop at the guard gate. Her power window glided soundlessly down.

"I've come to place an ad," she said before the guard could ask, then peered at the main building, an imposing red brick structure nestled within tall ivy-covered walls. Six stories high, its smoked glass windows overlooked Highways 8 and 163. "Is this the right place?"

"Sure is. Visitor's lot is the first section to your right."

She nodded her thanks and drove through. Apparently there weren't many visitors today, and she had her choice of spaces. After parking, she glanced back at the guard to see if he was watching.

He was.

Not wanting to arouse his suspicions, she got out and headed toward the curved pathway that led to the front doors. Walking slowly, she had time to wonder at Victor Griffith—ever the iconoclast and frequently outrageous—working in a staid environment like this.

As conservative as the buildings and grounds were, the lobby was even more so. Dark wood paneling and somber gray carpet brought to mind not reporters sniffing out a story but rather morticians determined not to offend the bereaved with even a single splash of color during the bleakest period of life.

At the center of the lobby sat a kiosk. This, Victor had told her, was where one placed a classified ad. And he had helpfully supplied her with a dummy ad purporting to offer Free Kittens to Good Homes.

When she'd protested that some little kid calling for a free kitten would be heartbroken to find the ad a hoax, he'd shrugged and said, "Life is hard."

Beyond the kiosk she could see a second guard sitting quietly but alert at a desk near the elevators. No one was allowed access to the upper floors without an appointment, and the keeper of the castle did not look as if he would be at all adverse to applying a little physical emphasis to company policy.

Sydney watched him as she crossed the lobby, half expecting him to challenge her right to be there, but his hooded eyes regarded her benignly, evidently having found her beneath concern.

Back in the parking lot a few minutes later, she popped the Mustang's hood. Pretending to have car trouble usually was good for thirty minutes to an hour of surveillance, and that, after all, was the reason she was here.

Victor estimated that Martina arrived at work between one-thirty and two, and it was now seventeen minutes past one. T minus thirteen and counting.

For now all she wanted was a look at—and photograph of—the young woman who'd captured Victor's heart. Later in the day she'd return and follow Ms. Saxon, presumably to her home. Once she had an address, the rest should prove to be fairly simple, if time-consuming.

Sydney went to the trunk and got out the small tool box she kept there. The tools included the usual assortment of sockets, ratchets, wrenches, and screwdrivers, along with the latest trick of her trade, a miniature camera that was hidden inside a fake Pepsi can. The camera shutter was operated by a trip mechanism which was activated when the can was tilted beyond an eighty degree angle.

She'd bought it on a whim at a convention and it had proven to be a valuable investment. Anyone who knew her knew she was as good as addicted to Pepsi, and it seemed somehow natural for her to have a can in her hand.

Placing the device on the fender beside her as she pretended to tinker with the engine, she would casually "take a drink" when Ms. Saxon arrived, capturing her subject on film.

Simple and unobtrusive.

"Problem?" a male voice said from behind her.

"The engine's missing a little," she said, glancing quickly over her shoulder to make sure it wasn't one of the security guards.

It wasn't. The man, middle-aged, bespectacled

and balding, was looking into the engine compartment with the apprehensive expression of the mechanically disinclined.

"I think it's a loose sparkplug wire," Sydney added. She straightened and reached for the red mechanic's towel she kept in the tool box, then began to wipe the grease off her hands. "Nothing serious."

"Well then, could I call anyone for you? The auto club or—"

"No thanks."

"—your husband, perhaps?" Behind thick lenses, the man's watery eyes held a hint of suggestiveness. "Because you've been, uh, stranded here for quite a little while now, and—"

From the corner of her eye, Sydney glimpsed a flash of powder blue. A late model Volkswagen Rabbit pulled into the parking lot, was waved through by the guard, and a second later turned down the aisle next to the one where Sydney was parked. As the car zipped by, Sydney saw enough of the license to verify that it was indeed a vanity plate, the last three letters of which were INA. She reached for the Pepsi can and was startled to feel the man's slightly sweaty hand closing around hers.

"I couldn't help noticing you," he said.

Sydney didn't care much for the sound of that, but at the moment she had other things on her mind. Furthermore, she wanted to avoid making a scene; she was here to watch, not *be* watched.

Martina Saxon had parked and gotten out of the Rabbit, and was walking in their direction. She was dressed casually, in white linen slacks and a black

25

turtleneck sweater, and the afternoon sun brought out the highlights in her honey blond hair.

There was something very familiar about her, Sydney thought. Very familiar.

"Would you like to have a cup of coffee with me?" the man asked.

"Never touch the stuff," Sydney answered, and wrested her hand and the Pepsi can from his grip. She lifted the can to her mouth and heard the soft click and whir of the camera autowind from within. "Bingo."

"Pardon?" The man, who was only an inch or so taller than her five foot four, moved closer. His breath smelled of cigarettes and peppermint. "Or we could go to a bar I know and have a drink."

Martina Saxon walked by a relatively scant fifteen feet away. Sydney tipped the can again, heard the click and whir. This close, she could see even more clearly what had attracted Victor: the high cheekbones, a peaches-and-cream complexion, and full, sensual lips. Very little make-up, Sydney judged, although she was far from an expert on such details.

"What do you say, then? A drink?"

A persistent bugger; one of the disadvantages of being a female in the business was the likelihood of drawing unwanted male attention at times like this. "Sorry, but if you don't get out of my face . . ."

The man's eyes narrowed, but he backed off, raising both hands in mock surrender. "No harm in asking," he said, an edge to his voice that hadn't been there before. He spun on his heel and hurried off.

Sydney frowned and watched him for a second or two—mildly surprised that he headed away from the building and not toward it—before turning in time to see Martina Saxon disappear through the employee entrance.

"Catch you later," she said.

Chapter Three

Back at the office, Sydney went directly into the darkroom to develop the photographs. She worked with an economy of effort born of long practice, and soon was taking the prints from the developer. Using tongs, she rinsed them in the stop-bath and then slid the photographs into the fixer tray. She set the digital timer for three minutes and turned away from the counter, stripping off her latex gloves.

And though there wasn't much room in which to do so, she began to pace. Irrational or not, she had a theory that she could jar things loose in her brain by pacing.

What needed jarring loose was why Martina Saxon had looked so familiar to her and from where. Her memory for names and faces was above average but not infallible, and all the way from Mission Valley to her office in University City she'd been rummaging through her mental attic.

To no avail. The best she'd been able to come up with thus far was where she *didn't* know Martina

Saxon from, and that included almost everywhere. They weren't neighbors, they didn't shop at the same stores or stand in line at the same bank, and hadn't smiled nervously at each other in the dentist's waiting room. The ten year difference in their ages pretty much eliminated having shared fingerpaints in kindergarten.

"Come on, Sydney, think," she directed herself. Her eyes came to rest on a slew of negatives that she'd been meaning to file but, slowdown or not, hadn't quite gotten around to.

She felt, suddenly, the restless stirring in the back of her mind that suggested she was close to an answer. That she hadn't met Martina Saxon, but had seen her photograph. More than once.

Depending on whose statistics you believed, San Diego was either the sixth or seventh largest city in the country, and finding any one face among the millions took some doing. The odds on the subject of one investigation showing up in the background of a picture taken of an earlier subject had to be a billion to one. As for showing up more than once . . . the odds would increase exponentially.

The digital timer was down to fifty-six seconds. Sydney hesitated, watched ten more seconds tick off, and decided to let well enough alone. If it came to her, fine. If not, what difference did it make? She hadn't been "hired" to uncover that particular detail . . .

She returned to the fixer tray, removed the prints and rinsed them in plain water before hanging them on the line to dry.

Dressed in black and white, photographed in

black and white, Ms. Saxon was a study in shades of gray.

When she'd finished straightening up the darkroom, she brought the photos to her desk and slipped them into the case file, deliberately avoiding looking at them for the time being. Then she went to the wall of shelves where she kept the hundreds of California phone and city directories she'd accumulated over the years, and after a moment, located the most recent San Diego phone book.

It didn't happen often, but sometimes she found what she was looking for in the most obvious places.

She opened it to the S's and began to flip through the pages when she heard a muffled thump at the door. Turning, she saw a shadow cross the pebbled-glass window and heard someone running along the wooden balcony that skirted the building and then down the stairs.

"What the hell?"

Outside, the sound of a racing engine and squealing tires drowned out the other traffic noise. Knowing she would probably be too late, Sydney ran to the window anyway, hoping to catch a glimpse of the fleeing vehicle.

All that remained was a thin cloud of blue smoke that hovered in the air for a few seconds before a truck lumbered through, dissipating the "evidence" in its wake.

She dropped the phone book, hurried to the office door and yanked it open. The breath caught in

30

her throat at the sight of blood. Dark red and clotted, the blood radiated out from the point of impact at the base of the door, and had splattered across the lower panels up to the level of the mail slot.

The doormat was saturated and there were fragments of what had probably been a balloon—a crude but effective method of delivery—caught in the weave. Blood had trickled from the door all the way to the balcony's edge, where it dripped off.

Sydney sat on her heels, partly to try to regain her equilibrium but primarily to see if there were shoe prints in the blood. There didn't appear to be.

Two suites down at the travel agency, the door opened and the secretary stood on the threshold as if frozen, pale-faced and wide-eyed at the sight of the gore. Her mouth opened and closed half a dozen times before she managed to gasp, "Mr. Porter!"

The owner of Porter's Ports of Call stepped around his secretary and, coffee cup in hand, surveyed the scene. He shook his head, took a sip of coffee, and gave Sydney a sympathetic smile. "Think you'll be needing to get out of town?"

"I don't scare this easily," she said, "but I might consider getting mad."

Chapter Four

In spite of the afternoon's distractions, at a quarter to six Sydney had positioned herself to follow Martina Saxon as she left work. Illegally parked a hundred yards or so west of the newspaper complex entrance, she watched a steady stream of cars exit the lot.

Almost all of the cars turned left and east onto Camino de la Reina, and the string of tail lights imparted a red glow to the fine mist that had moved inland after sunset. Moisture beaded on the windshield, and Sydney reached to turn on the wipers.

There, three cars back from the street. The Rabbit was sandwiched between a Union-Tribune van and a sleek Jaguar XJE with a cellular phone antenna. In the otherworldly light from a nearby streetlamp, Sydney could make out a single silhouette.

Martina was alone.

Sydney turned the key in the ignition and the Mustang engine came to life. She shifted into first, eased up on the clutch and let the car glide forward.

Timing was absolutely of the essence in conducting a successful tail, and she wanted to reach the intersection just after Martina completed her turn, then fall in behind her.

As luck would have it, the van in front of the Rabbit made a right, its headlights momentarily blinding her while its bulky form blocked the Rabbit from view. She took a chance and accelerated anyway, then had to brake sharply as the Jaguar cut in front of her, hot on the Rabbit's rear bumper.

Sydney flashed her bright lights, both to show her annoyance and to catch a glimpse of the driver of the Jag. The driver definitely was male, and he appeared to be talking on the phone.

"Typical," she said, then looked ahead to Ms. Saxon's car which was entering the north-bound freeway on-ramp. The Jag followed suit, still hugging the Rabbit's bumper.

Either they were together and didn't want to become separated, Sydney thought, or he was an extremely aggressive driver, begrudging every second wasted. For Victor's sake, she hoped it was the latter.

Freeway traffic was only moderately heavy for the hour, and it was moving quickly, so she forgot about the Jag—which vanished into the fast lane—and concentrated on keeping the Rabbit in view. The object of Victor's affection was pretty aggressive herself, zipping from lane to lane, passing slower vehicles and jockeying for position with other speed demons. When the interchange to I-15 came up, the Rabbit cut haphazardly across three lanes to reach it, forcing Sydney to do the same.

After a quick glance in the rearview mirror to check for flashing lights, she tightened her grip on the wheel and increased her speed, the better to keep up. It occurred to her that perhaps Martina Saxon knew she was being tailed, but experience told her that even people with good reason to suspect they might be followed seldom could detect an actual tail.

The only time Sydney had ever been made was ten years ago, when she was still in training at a large investigative firm in Los Angeles. The subject was a Wally Cox look-alike who was in the process of embezzling funds from his employer, a defense sub-contractor.

Given the assignment on a Friday, she'd spent a frustrating weekend tracking him as he criss-crossed the city by bus. He got on and off so many buses that Sydney was ready to push him under one just to stop having to breathe the exhaust fumes. Finally, on Sunday morning when he left his apartment, he came over to her car, tapped on the passenger window and, when she rolled it down, handed her a bus schedule with his route marked in fluorescent yellow high-lighter.

Later, when he was arrested, they found his apartment stacked to the ceiling with mystery novels. Hard-boiled, soft-boiled or cozies, he read them all, and he extended his thanks to her through his attorney for allowing him to live out a favorite fantasy.

Her boss at the time had been amused, but it had been a while before she'd worked another tail.

Right now, though, she would welcome a map;

Martina Saxon had exited the freeway onto one of the winding, curvy roads that the North County was famous for, made two or three turns after that, and Sydney hadn't a hint as to where they were.

The road signs — when there were any — were angled wrong to be read in a hurry, or else were obscured by overhanging branches of trees. She didn't dare slow down and fall behind or she was sure to lose the Rabbit.

Another sharp right turn onto a road which quickly narrowed to one lane before beginning to climb.

Sydney turned off her headlights. She had a hunch that this was a private road, and if she was right, Martina Saxon would surely begin to wonder who was following her. And if she was right, the road would dead-end, which, in theory at least, meant she couldn't be shaken.

The moon was three-quarters full, and between its illumination and the Rabbit's tail lights a distance ahead, Sydney managed to keep the Mustang from running off the pavement. On either side, the hedges formed a high, thick wall which she could not see beyond. The farther she drove, the nearer the bushes came to the road, as though they were closing in.

The effect was oppressive and disorienting. It was easy to imagine that dark growth entwined around her, sharp, brittle branches clutching and scratching at her like skeletal fingers . . .

It was, she thought, the kind of place where she would prefer not to run out of gas.

The car crested the hill then, and the paved road

gave way to gravel. Gradually the shrubbery thinned and the road widened again. Then she saw the house.

It sat at the center of the graded hilltop, lit dramatically by dozens of spotlights hidden in the lush surrounding landscape. Hacienda-style, with brilliant white columned terraces and red-tiled roofs, the house sprawled over the better part of an acre.

Whatever Sydney had expected, it hadn't been this. She braked to a stop, then leaned forward, arms draped over the steering wheel as she surveyed the grounds. The Rabbit was nowhere in sight, but one of the doors of the eight-car garage was open and a moment later, Martina Saxon walked out and headed toward the house along a stone path. The garage door lowered.

"Saxon," Sydney mused aloud, and all at once in her mind, things clicked into place like the pins within a lock cylinder.

Martina Saxon had to be one of *the* Saxons. And this had to be Villa Saxon, the family estate.

Headed by matriarch Penelope Day Saxon, the family was one of the wealthiest and most influential in Southern California, or indeed the state. Born to money and later wed to it, Miss Penelope at age seventy-five still graced the pages of society news, holding court with the privileged even as she reputedly wielded her considerable power to control the vast Saxon land holdings.

The society columns — a secret passion of hers — were where Sydney had seen Martina before; the young woman had no doubt appeared in countless photographs of the city's true elite. Dressed in white satin, blond hair swept up off her slender neck and adorned with the Day or Saxon heirloom jewels, her type of cool beauty would draw the eye in any debutante crowd.

Martina in her natural habitat was seriously out of Victor's league.

The question was, what was Martina Saxon doing in the slightly grubby world of journalism?

And why didn't Victor know who she was?

Chapter Five

Victor Griffith licked the salsa off his bony fingers and frowned. "She's a what?"

"A Saxon, as in Saxon Land Development. As in Saxon and Associates. As in Saxon Global Investments." Seeing the blank look in his eyes, she added, "As in filthy stinking rich."

"Martina?"

Sydney nodded. "I don't know yet where she fits in on the family tree, but she's not your average girl-next-door. Not by a long shot."

The fish taco in Victor's hand continued to drip salsa onto its yellow wax-paper wrapping. The table was littered with similar wrappers and after a moment, he dropped the taco on the pile and gathered all of the refuse into a greasy ball which he tossed in the general direction of the trash can. "This isn't what I expected," he said.

Sydney said nothing but, shivering, zipped up her jacket and put her hands in her pockets to warm them. The weather, mild during the day, was downright chilly at night. Of all of Victor's favorite haunts, why had he chosen the one with outdoor seating at which to have a midnight snack?

"So much for the family history." His smile was rueful. "And here I was worried about ax murderers."

"Yes, well . . ."

"She doesn't act like a rich—" He swallowed the expletive and ducked his head, trying unsuccessfully to hide a guilty expression.

Victor had never made a secret of the fact that he had an ingrained distrust and even hatred of the wealthy that went far deeper than the disguised envy that most people felt. Those whose fortunes were inherited garnered the lion's share of his scorn.

But not all of it. Notoriously frugal, he often swore that he'd give the biggest party the city had ever seen when and if Trump went bankrupt. A going under party, he called it.

Feeling as he did, it must be painful to find himself in love with the enemy . . .

"I wouldn't jump to conclusions," Sydney said. "Not everyone with money is a bitch."

The corners of his mouth twitched downward. "I dare say you're right; most of them are bastards."

"Victor." A car sped by and Sydney braced for the rush of cold air on her unprotected neck. "What I'm curious about is why you didn't know."

"Know what?"

"Who she is. I mean, how does someone keep a thing like that a secret?"

"Sydney, Sydney, Sydney." He shook his head and gave her a condescending smile. "Surely you've learned by now that you can damned well too fool all of the people all of the time. If you work at it."

"Actually, I haven't learned." She subscribed to the theory that there were no absolute secrets, that someone, somewhere, always knew the truth.

He reached across the table and chucked her under the chin. "You've got to get out more."

She suppressed a flash of annoyance. "Her photograph has been in *your* newspaper dozens of times. How could people that she worked with every day not recognize her?"

"Well," he said evenly, "in the first place, she's not there every day."

"You know what I mean."

"And when she is, she works primarily on the fifth floor—"

"In the morgue?"

"We prefer to call it the library. A morgue is so . . . lifeless. And good stories never die, you know; they only wait to be resurrected."

"If you say so. Still, even if she wasn't in editorial, you would think that once in six months she'd have shared an elevator with the society columnist—"

"Works from home," he interrupted.

"Or a photographer who'd been assigned to a regatta or whatever—"

"Nope. Shutterbugs only show on payday, and even then they're in and out so fast you'd need a film speed setting of sixteen hundred to capture their smiling, acned faces for posterity."

"Then what about you?" she persisted. "Don't you read your own newspaper?"

"I only read my own work."

That she believed. "Fine. No one recognized her. But why would she hide her connections? Especially working in a field where who you know is more important than what you know?"

Victor rubbed at a greasy spot on the table with his thumb and then wiped his thumb absently on his pant leg before meeting her eyes. "I don't care about any of that, Sydney. I guess I don't even care if she's rich. I just want to know . . . if she's seeing anybody."

She regarded him for a moment, uncertain of how to respond. Some part of her wanted to warn him that he was setting himself up for a fall, but it was hardly her place to play mother hen, and she doubted if he'd welcome interference from her or anyone else.

You can't choose who you love, she thought, and said: "All right. I'll see what else I can find out about Martina."

A little of the light returned to his eyes. "Thanks, Sydney. I really do appreciate it."

She stood up and started to leave, but then hesitated. The cool air invaded the warmth of her jacket, tracing chills up her spine. "I hope this works out for you."

But Victor was staring off into space, oblivious. "She drives a Volkswagen, for crying out loud."

Chapter Six

Her apartment was dark and as silent as a tomb, and that pleased her no end.

She liked coming home to the slightly stuffy air, and to the blinking red light on her answering machine. She liked coming home to a late dinner of cold macaroni and cheese, eaten with her fingers while standing in front of the open refrigerator door.

It pleased her that it was well after midnight and she'd been too busy to get her mail, and that the evening newspaper would be tossed straight into the recycling bin because she hadn't time to read it.

All of it meant she was working.

"You're addicted to your job," her mother observed at regular intervals.

Sydney had given up denying it; work was her focus and passion. Particularly now, when her personal life was so damned confusing . . .

She hung her jacket and purse on the hook inside the closet door and crossed the room to the couch. After hitting rewind on the answering machine, she sat down and kicked off her shoes.

Her eyelids were feeling a little heavy—it had been weeks since she'd stayed up late enough to catch even the early news—but she savored the sensation. And there was no way she would let a mild case of exhaustion run her off to bed.

The answering machine clicked, fully rewound, and she hit the play button with a sigh.

"Sydney," her mother's voice said. "I just wanted to remind you to come to dinner on Wednesday. I'm fixing a roast. And deep-dish apple pie with cinnamon crumb topping. Let's see, what else was I going to say? Oh, now I've forgotten. You know I hate this machine of yours . . . always cutting me off in mid-thought . . . so I'll beat the rude little bugger and say good-bye."

Sydney laughed softly and leaned her head back against the cushion. It wouldn't hurt to close her eyes for a minute while she listened to her messages.

"Sydney. It's your mother again. Wear something nice, okay? That pretty red dress, you know the one. And listen, honey, I know it's none of my business, but I want to talk to you about Ethan."

Ethan. She hadn't seen him since Thanksgiving. Was he still upset with her? Sooner or later, they'd have to talk, but—

"Hello kid," the next message began.

Sydney smiled. There was nothing of Lieutenant Travis in the intimate tone of Mitch's voice.

"I guess you're working, so I don't have to apologize for doing the same. We caught a double homicide a couple of hours ago. Looks domestic so far, but who the hell knows these days. If we can clear it, I'll see you tomorrow night. If not, I—what?"

43

He evidently had covered the receiver, because what followed sounded muffled. She opened her eyes and glanced at the answering machine.

"Damn," he said then, a cop again. "Gotta go."

Listening to the dial tone, Sydney thought about the lives that had been or soon would be disrupted by the deaths of two people somewhere in the city. Domestic or not, the shock waves resulting from homicide radiated along fault lines far from the epicenter.

The machine beeped, and a male voice said, "I hope this is the right number for . . . is it Sydney Bryant?"

Someone selling something, she thought, closing her eyes again.

"Miss Bryant, you don't know me," the man said, "but I feel that I should warn you . . ."

The voice trailed off and she could hear only the labored sound of his breathing. As though, she thought, he'd been running.

Intrigued, she reached over and turned up the volume. The tape had picked up random background noises—the drone of traffic, the high-pitched squeal of brakes, and the annoying throbbing bass of a passing boom box—which suggested that the call had been made from a pay phone.

"Come on," she urged. The answering machine had a forty second limit before it disconnected the caller, and most of that had passed.

The man cleared his throat. "Just watch yourself, Miss Bryant," he rasped, and hung up.

Another beep, indicating a subsequent call, but

this time there was only the sound of the receiver being gently replaced and the dial tone thereafter.

Sydney frowned, drumming her fingers on the arm of the couch. The machine played on through several more hang-ups before reaching the white noise hiss of blank tape. It took several minutes more before the tape reached the end, triggering the automatic rewind.

She got up and sat on her heels in front of the telephone table, opening the plastic cover and watching the tiny spools spin. When they came to a stop, she removed the cassette, opened the table drawer and took out a fresh one which she inserted into the machine.

Straightening, she went directly to the closet and slipped the tape with its cryptic warning into her shoulder bag. Tomorrow she'd put it in her safe deposit box at the bank.

Up till now, she'd taken a relatively relaxed attitude about the calls she'd been getting, the "wrong numbers." Even the vandalism at her office this afternoon had not been enough to change that, although she immediately assumed that the incidents were connected. She also assumed that the vandalism signaled an escalation of the harassment.

She'd kept her cool largely because, after the shock had worn off, she'd been able to determine that it wasn't real blood that had splattered her door. As imitation blood went, it was better than most, but still not good enough; some months back, a friend who worked in the city's crime lab had given her a can of Luminal, which, though the least sensitive color reaction test, was specific enough to verify the presence of blood.

Knowing that, she'd decided against filing a police report. The first question the police would ask was one she'd asked herself over and over again: "Do you have any idea of who might be doing these things?"

She didn't have a clue. Which, as she saw it, meant that reporting either incident would be an exercise in futility, because there was really nothing she could tell them beyond the sketchy facts.

But now, with this call . . . now the situation was getting out of hand; The man had called her at *home,* in spite of the fact that she had an unlisted number. And despite his implied concern for her safety, it could be that his real intention was to frighten her.

That simply wasn't going to happen.

What would happen was that she would compile a history and timetable of what had occurred thus far, documenting the harassment. Then she would search the office for the old answering machine she'd used before she could afford an answering service so that she could get the woman's voice on tape as well.

And when she finished with Victor's case, she would find out who was behind all of this, with or without Pac Bell's help.

Chapter Seven

Tuesday

By noon, Sydney had amassed a stack of articles on the Saxons, using a microfiche copier in the central library at the University of California, San Diego. She'd also run out of change to feed into the slot, having gone through two rolls of dimes and every coin, save pennies, in her shoulder bag.

Judging by the amount of material generated in just the last fifteen months, a Saxon sneezing was considered newsworthy by the local media.

The articles, taken from the *Union*—for some reason, UCSD didn't archive the *Tribune*—included columns from the financial pages as well as society news and, curiously, a two-inch item from the Metro section on the arrest of Randall Day, Penelope Day Saxon's brother, for reckless driving on the Fourth of July.

It would be better, Sydney thought, to review the articles in the silence and privacy of her office, so she gathered the copies and slid them into her leather satchel. After checking her jacket pocket for her car keys, she got up and left the microfiche copier to a rather wild-eyed student who'd been pacing anxiously behind her for the last fifteen minutes.

Outside, the air was fragrant with the medicinal scent of eucalyptus trees, thousands of which covered the campus. She walked the short distance to where she'd parked and was relieved to see that there were still a few minutes left on the meter. As she unlocked the door, she noticed a late model burgundy Chrysler which had been idling in the circular turnabout to the left of the library begin to move forward, coming in her direction.

Parking spaces were precious commodities on campus, and she expected the driver to stake his claim by positioning himself a car-length behind her, blocking off the other space-seekers. She glanced in his direction as she swung the door open and stuck the satchel behind the seat.

But the Chrysler didn't stop, and as it drove past, the driver looked directly at her and winked.

She recognized him as the man who'd tried to pick her up yesterday at the *Union-Tribune*.

His glasses caught the light then, obscuring his eyes, but he gave her a jaunty wave, gunned the engine and took off, the Chrysler's tires shedding rubber on the pavement.

Taken aback, Sydney could only stare after him until the horn of an impatient parking space hunter reclaimed her attention.

At the office, Sydney organized the material she

had collected into a binder, in chronological order, with the most recent articles in the front. When she finished, she began to page through the copies, eyes straining with the effort of reading the tiny print.

Most of the articles were standard society news issue, and the photographs that accompanied them usually featured men in tuxedos and women in designer originals at this or that charity event. Whether by chance or design, these beautiful people were captured on film smiling at the camera with a hint of disdain, their perfectly sculpted noses marginally up-turned.

Fluff, Victor would call it, but there were things to be learned.

Flipping back and forth among the pages, Sydney was able to put together at least one branch of the family tree, thus determining that Martina was the daughter of Jared and Amanda Saxon, and a grandchild of Penelope Day Saxon. She was the youngest of three children, the eldest of whom was a brother named David, who had recently gotten engaged. Owen, the middle child, was blessed with Greek god looks, marred somewhat by his petulant expression.

She learned, too, that in the six months that Martina had been working at the newspaper—and capturing Victor's heart—the young woman had been photographed on at least a dozen occasions with a variety of escorts. The men in question were immaculately groomed and tailored, and oozed self-assurance.

Try as she might, Sydney could not fit Victor into the picture, what with his off-the-tall-rack sports jackets and frayed pant cuffs. Her imagination faltered at the point where he would join in raising a glass of Dom Perignon to the continued well-being of his fat-cat host.

Some things were better left unexamined.

And she learned a few things which probably had nothing to do with anything, but which she found of interest nonetheless.

Earlier in the year, the vice-president of property acquisitions at Saxon Land Development had been dismissed for the systematic sexual harassment of virtually every female the company employed.

"I don't know how he could expend all that energy," Jared Saxon was quoted as saying, presumably tongue-in-cheek, "and still play a decent round of golf."

Charges were pending.

Meanwhile, at Saxon Global, a consultant hired to streamline the process for international monetary exchanges had made expenditures of a different sort, tapping into the company's computerized accounting program and directing bank interest payments to be made to a dummy corporation he'd set up in Brazil.

The consultant had fled soon after. The Saxon family, both immediate and extended, was vacationing in Europe when the theft was revealed, and in their absence, the office of attorney Boyd Harrington had released a terse statement to the press.

"Saxon Global will recover the missing funds," the statement read, "one way or another."

That sounded like a threat, Sydney thought. Unusual coming from a high-powered lawyer like Harrington, whose reputation around town held that he was a model of restraint and discretion.

And, finally, she learned where Martina would be this very evening; at The Tides, an exclusive club in the Marina, attending the Autumn Festival, one of the highlights of the social season.

It occurred to her that holding the Autumn Festival when winter was dead upon them showed how far removed the blue bloods were from real life.

Obviously she would be unable to shadow Martina all evening, but at least she could see which elegant young man would escort her tonight.

Chapter Eight

The private road that led to the Saxon estate looked markedly different by daylight, even if the light was fading. Sydney lifted her foot off the gas pedal, relying on the engine's idle to ease the Mustang forward.

Last night the bushes along the roadside had seemed almost threatening; today they offered a place of concealment from which to watch the residents of Villa Saxon as they left for the Autumn Festival.

In the darkness, the thick growth of bushes, shrubs and trees had appeared as impenetrable as a granite wall, but she saw now that there were a number of hollows and recesses deep enough to back the car into. With luck, the coming of dusk would further shield her from sight.

It was chancy to hide on private property; there was always the risk that she'd be discovered trespassing, and if that happened, she wouldn't have a legal leg to stand on. She'd considered parking a distance away and walking up—she'd certainly be less visible on foot—but she felt safer in the car.

If challenged, she could drive a lot faster than she could run. And her Smith and Wesson .38 Special was locked in the glove compartment, not that she really expected to need it.

She had reached the crest of the hill and was looking for a place to turn around when she saw the perfect hiding spot: a willow tree off to the side of the road a hundred yards ahead. Its branches formed a canopy, reaching nearly to the ground.

Sydney glanced toward Villa Saxon, even more spectacular by day, and then drove off the pavement onto the soft dirt shoulder. Although she wasn't doing three miles an hour, dust swirled up from the tires, a fine cloud trailing her to the willow tree.

She could only hope no one was watching.

When she had angled the car so that she could see both the road and the mansion below, she turned off the motor and settled in to wait.

The three-quarter moon had long since risen before the first of the cars left the estate grounds. She watched headlights approach, and as the car drew near she saw that it was a white Mercedes limousine. There was enough ambient light to see the driver, proper in his uniform and cap, but not the passenger.

Of course not the passenger, who would be behind a smoked glass partition.

"Wonderful," she said, rapping the side of her head with her knuckles. "Why didn't you *think* about limos? Why didn't you *think* about partitions?"

If the Saxons all were going to the Autumn Festival by limousine, she'd wasted her time coming out here. She'd have a dandy view of the hired help, but not much else. Martina could drive by with the Vienna Boys Choir and she wouldn't know.

Down the hill, a second pair of headlights flicked on. Then a third.

Sydney crossed her fingers.

The second car, thank heavens, was a Cadillac Fleetwood. And its windows weren't smoked, allowing her a clear view of Jared and Amanda Saxon as they drove by. Five seconds later a low-slung Ferrari followed.

Owen Saxon was driving stiff-armed, his hands at one and eleven o'clock on the steering wheel. Even in the dim light, Sydney could make out the rage on his face that mirrored his tense posture.

There wasn't time to wonder at the cause of his anger; a fourth car was rapidly closing the distance between it and the Ferrari. Sydney ducked slightly as headlights flashed momentarily in her direction — the car had started to slide on the gravel section of the road before the driver regained control — and looked up again to see that the vehicle was a Jeep with a canvas top.

She couldn't identify the driver through the mud-splattered windshield, but she did note that whoever it was appeared to be alone.

As reckless as the Jeep driver was driving, she could understand that.

A minute or two passed before the next car came along. The interior light in the Volvo station wagon was on, and Sydney watched as the driver, a woman who looked to be in her early sixties, held a piece of paper up to read.

"Who's this?" Sydney wondered aloud, unable to connect a name with the rather stern-featured face. The woman's gray hair was drawn tight in a bun, and she wore a plain black cloth coat. Her mouth quirked in a frown as she crumpled the paper into a ball and flung it out of the open window.

Sydney watched after the Volvo as it disappeared over the crest. The woman probably was one of the household help, but even so, Sydney found herself curious about the display of temper.

Again, there wasn't opportunity to reflect on it or to attempt to retrieve the note, because two more sets of headlights were making their way up this side of the hill. Even before it reached her, Sydney recognized the first car as a Jaguar XJE by its body shape, and she wondered briefly if this was the same Jag that had cut her off last night. She vaguely recalled that it had been dark in color, as was this one.

Not that that proved anything; there wasn't exactly a scarcity of Jags hereabouts.

There were two people in the XJE and she looked at the woman first, half expecting it to be Martina. But the woman, although blonde, was some twenty years older. Her jawline had sagged with age, a fact the woman tried unsuccessfully to disguise with a scarf.

The man driving the Jag was none other than Boyd Harrington, Esquire. The toast of the legal community was holding a white handkerchief to his right cheek. And he wasn't dabbing at his face, the way a person would to soak up perspiration, but pressing firmly, as though to staunch the flow of blood.

Sydney reluctantly turned her attention to the car behind Harrington's Jag. Another Mercedes, but this one a 450SL convertible with the top down.

Randall Day looked resplendent in his tuxedo, his top hat pulled firmly down on his head and held by one hand as he steered with the other. Even with her windows up, Sydney could hear the rousing shit-kicking, boot-stomping music that blared from the stereo. Randall Day, bon vivant, who had dined with kings and princes around the world, was singing along at the top of his lungs.

". . . drop-kick your heart right out the door," she heard as the Benz passed.

A song obviously headed up the charts with a bullet, Sydney thought, and smiled. At least Great Uncle Randall was in a good mood tonight.

She looked toward the house, then pressed the button on her watch to illuminate its face. Seven minutes to seven p.m. The Festival would presumably begin any minute now, and although she could appreciate the concept of being fashionably late, she wondered how much longer Martina would be.

Unless, of course, Martina had already driven by in the limousine. An even money bet, she thought, but a prospect she was unwilling to concede, since

56

the most likely occupant of the limo was Miss Penelope herself.

Yet another set of headlights blinked on, and Sydney watched their slow progress up the hill. Whoever this was didn't drive like Martina, but maybe it was one of Victor's competitors.

The car wasn't the Rabbit, Sydney noted with some disappointment. She suppressed a sigh—she was supposed to have dinner with Mitch this evening and didn't want to stand him up—and stared at the approaching vehicle, trying to make out who its occupants were.

David Saxon, the first born of Miss Penelope's grandchildren. He had his father's square jaw and his mother's serenity . . . or was it a lack of affect, as the psychiatrists would say?

Beside him sat his fiance, Felice McDaniel. In contrast to their engagement announcement photograph, in which Felice had dressed as a Southern belle in deference to her ancestry, tonight she looked very much the part of a 1920's flapper. She wore her dark hair short and slicked back, in almost a masculine style.

David reached over to light her cigarette, and in the flickering glow, Sydney took in the dark red lipstick, the fine-penciled eyebrows, and the alabaster white of her skin.

Then they too were gone.

Time passed.

When the digital numbers on her watch read

seven-thirty, Sydney reached for the key in the ignition.

Martina had not left the house, or if she had, Sydney had missed her. The lights in the house that had been on half an hour ago were still on, and all eight garage doors were closed.

Not a creature was stirring, indeed.

Maybe the limousine had been hired by Martina's escort. Or maybe Miss Penelope was feeling under the weather—she was seventy-five years old, after all—and the matriarch had urged her granddaughter to make use of the splendid vehicle in place of the Rabbit.

Or maybe Martina was the one who'd fallen ill. Or maybe she'd forgotten all about the Festival, caught up in her work at the newspaper morgue.

If she tried, Sydney could come up with a hundred maybes, but only one stuck in her mind: *Maybe I'd better go take a look.*

Chapter Nine

Her intention had been to follow the circular driveway past the sprawling hacienda, then stop in front of the garage, tip-toe over and peek in the narrow bunker-type windows on each of the doors. If the Rabbit was parked inside, she would return to her hiding spot, wait another fifteen minutes for Martina to show, and if she didn't, call it a night. If the Rabbit wasn't in the garage, she would leave immediately.

Her intention was forgotten as she neared the house and saw that the front door was standing open.

Without taking her eyes from the door, Sydney pressed the power window controls, lowering both windows. She applied the brakes and when the car had come to a stop, turned off the engine and listened.

Crickets serenaded the moon. Wind whispered through the palm trees that lined the drive. Water spilled from a marble nymph's cupped hands into the small pond that surrounded the fountain near the front terrace.

There were no other sounds.

Sydney removed the key from the ignition and got out of the car. The gravel crunched beneath her feet as she walked toward the open door. Light spilled from the door only to be swallowed by the darkness . . .

As she reached the black stone path that led to the entry, Sydney hesitated, unable to shake a sudden certainty that something was wrong here.

Turn back, an inner voice said.

She ignored it. After drawing cool air into her lungs, she continued on. Stepping lightly, her Nikes soundless, she reached the raised porch. From here she could see into the foyer, which appeared deserted.

"Hello?" She stopped at the threshold, listening again. There was no response.

From somewhere within the house came the cadence of seconds being measured off by a grandfather clock. And the low hum of central heating, trying to compensate for the influx of chill night air.

That and her pulse quickening in her ears was all that Sydney heard.

She took a step inside, her shoes squeaking on the polished rosewood floor. The foyer smelled of lemon oil and hot scented wax. There were three arched doorways, to the left, to the right, and directly ahead. All three were open to one degree or another.

Looking to her right, she could see into an

enormous tri-level living room with vaulted ceilings and a massive fieldstone fireplace, embers glowing within. The furnishings were modern, earth tone fabrics and wood accents. On one of the tables sat a glass decanter filled with an amber liquid, bracketed by two brandy snifters.

Through the living room, she could make out a hallway which evidently led to another part of the house. The hallway itself was dark, but somewhere beyond it lights were on, evidenced by a barely perceptible lessening of the shadows.

Sydney frowned. For some reason, she did not relish the prospect of walking down that hall.

So she wouldn't, at least not without considering the alternatives. She glanced to her left. The second door was only a third of the way open, and the chandelier in the foyer cast but a thin wedge of light into the room. Not much of an improvement over the dark hallway.

That left the door straight ahead. There was an odd quality to the light coming from beyond the last door. Kind of a muted blue light, common perhaps to special effects wizards, but out of place here.

Sydney thought of the zillion or so scary movies she'd seen growing up, and the child in her felt the tingling apprehensiveness that had always felt delicious when she was safe at home, her parents upstairs asleep. Even though she'd whispered urgent warnings to the hero and heroine not to go into that place with the eerie light, she would've been disappointed if they hadn't.

And although she was beginning to have bad feelings about remaining in the house, she'd be disappointed with herself if she gave in to her fears.

The door led into a central courtyard. Glancing up, she saw the metal framework and glass panels that enclosed the space. Track lighting directed spotlights at an exotic variety of leafy plants — horticulture wasn't her strong suit — that grew in profusion around the waterfalls that supplied three spas and a clover-shaped swimming pool.

Sydney felt a tightening in her stomach as she looked at the pool, which was partially hidden by the greenery. The underwater lights were on, and she thought she saw something floating, something that looked very much like a woman's hair.

The pulse in her throat grew more rapid.

The ceramic-tiled surface was slick from the misting machines which watered the plants, and she had to be careful as she walked along the curved pathway that led to the pool. Walking slowly also gave her a chance to come up with an alternate explanation for what she'd seen, or thought she'd seen.

A leafy fern fallen into the water. A trick of the light. Or an overactive imagination.

She detected movement out of the corner of her

eye and stopped abruptly, then let her breath out in a sigh when she realized that there were a dozen or so sliding patio doors that led into the courtyard from all sides. She'd caught a glimpse of her own reflection in the glass.

Bracing herself, she went on, this time watching her image as it flickered from pane to pane. Then she reached the wooden deck that surrounded the pool and saw that it hadn't been her imagination.

A woman's body floated facedown in the shallow water of the pool, her hair fanned out in a halo around her head. She wore only a white slip, slashed and tinged red with blood from several stab wounds in her back. Blood had clouded the water around her—Sydney thought absurdly of sharks—and some of it had flowed like hot lava along the bottom of the pool to the drain.

A curious numbness came over her, as though someone had injected her with Novocaine, and her ribcage constricted, making it difficult to breathe. More than that, her peripheral vision seemed to have failed her, the background fading to blackness, so that all she could see was the woman's body.

Even without seeing the woman's face, Sydney knew it was Martina Saxon.

Chapter Ten

The first deputy to arrive sequestered her in one of the changing rooms along the north side of the courtyard to await the Homicide team for questioning. After drawing the drapes across the sliding glass door that opened into the pool area — the presumed crime scene — he left her alone with a stern look she interpreted to mean, *stay put*.

Thirty minutes passed during which she heard a great deal of banging and slamming of doors, along with the clamor of footsteps. They were searching, she realized belatedly, to see if there was anyone else on the premises.

Anyone else, as in whoever had murdered Martina Saxon.

Odd that it hadn't occurred to her before now that she might not have been alone in the house. The hair on the back of her neck prickled at the thought, and she made an effort to clear her mind. She could ill afford to have her instincts blunted by shock; another delayed reaction might exact a substantial price.

Sydney became aware then of muffled voices beyond the glass wall, punctuated by an occasional burst of static from someone's mobile radio. Staring at the narrow opening between the drapes, she saw flash after photoflash as still pictures were being taken.

Her reserve of compliance pretty much used up, she moved to the window, parting the drapes slightly. She counted an even dozen men gathered in the courtyard, three of whom looked to be actually doing their jobs while the others observed.

They were removing the body from the pool.

Sydney closed her eyes momentarily, sickened by the sight. She had seen death in many forms these past ten years, but familiarity did not equal acceptance. It never seemed to get easier . . . and it shouldn't.

Experience told her that her dreams would be haunted by the lifeless way Martina's head fell back as they lifted her from the water, by eyes that stared unseeing, and by the bloodless pallor of her flesh.

A body bag had been placed beside the pool, and they laid her on the thick plastic. A deputy coroner squatted beside the body, drew on a pair of disposable gloves, and reached into his black bag. He withdrew the long metal thermometer used to take the core body temperature to aid in determining the time of death.

Sydney averted her eyes, searching other faces

in the vain hope that she could distract herself from what the coroner was about to do. Their expressions varied from mild interest to absolute boredom.

Behind her, the door opened.

"Miss Bryant?" a voice rumbled.

She turned to see a huge Clydesdale of a man filling every dimension of the doorway. The bristly brown hair of his flat-top cleared the door-frame by at most a centimeter, and his meaty shoulders just missed being wedged in tight. A massive hand unfastened his suede jacket, the buttons of which were straining at their threads.

Crafty blue eyes regarded her beneath Andy Rooney eyebrows. His thin lips were tight in a frown, and furrows bracketed his mouth.

She let the drape close. "Yes."

He came into the room, swung the door shut behind him. She had a moment to wonder why the floor hadn't quaked beneath him before he spoke again.

"Name's Grant." He flipped open a leather bi-fold to display his badge. "I'm in charge."

She didn't doubt that.

"I understand that you were the one who discovered the body. Is that right?"

"Yes." She swallowed the 'sir,' sensing that he would mistake it as weakness on her part.

"And you're some kind of private investigator, I hear. Is that right?"

"Yes. My I.D. is in the car—"

He waved it off. "We can play show-and-tell later. Would you mind telling me what the hell you were doing here tonight?"

She gave him an abbreviated version of the specifics of the case and the progress she'd made during the past two days as he wandered through the room—made smaller by his presence—and looked everywhere but at her.

"When I saw the front door standing open," she concluded, "I thought I'd better take a look."

"Is that right? You know—" he peered through the gap in the drapes "—most folks would have called the cops in a situation like that."

Sydney didn't respond.

"If only to cover their own asses, if you take my meaning. Heaven forbid they find themselves suspected in a murder just because they stick their noses where they don't belong."

He couldn't have been more obviously baiting her than if he'd waved a mackerel in her face. She waited until he glanced in her direction, then smiled.

"Is that right?" she said.

His eyebrows knit together, forming a solid line. "I wouldn't wise off if I were you. I am not in a good mood here, Miss Bryant, and my job's difficult enough without having to go through amateur hour with a make-believe wannabe."

It wasn't the first time she'd been on the receiv-

67

ing end of some cop's disregard for P.I.'s, but even so, she felt her color begin to rise. Warring factions in her brain battled over a suitable response, but for a change, the diplomatic side won.

"I apologize if I came off as flippant or unprofessional," she said coolly, lifting her chin, "but I don't think either of us will benefit from going for each other's throat."

A corner of his mouth twitched. "As if you could reach mine—"

There was a knock at the door a microsecond before it opened and another plainclothesman leaned in. "Dwight, you'd better come. The family is here."

"What the fuck? How'd *they* get word?"

"Your guess is as good as mine, but they're here and they're not happy campers, to say the least. The shit is about to fly."

Grant pointed a beefy index finger at Sydney. "You stay here, understand?"

She nodded.

He thundered out, and this time Sydney felt the floorboards vibrate.

Midnight came and went. Sydney gave up looking at her watch—as she'd done every five minutes for the past four hours—and curled up on the cushioned rattan lounge to try and make the best of a bad situation by getting a little rest.

Sleep eluded her, but she closed her eyes determinedly and tried not to think.

She failed. Images bombarded her from all sides, with even the most innocuous thought leading inevitably back to the unsettling specter of death.

An hour ago, a deputy had brought her a cup of coffee from the operations truck set up outside. The deputy hadn't been willing or able to answer her question as to how much longer she'd have to wait, but glancing around him, she'd seen the stretcher bearing Martina's body—now covered by a dark blue velvet shroud—as it rolled by.

Shortly thereafter, she'd opened the door, hoping to find someone willing to allow her the use of a phone and had seen, instead, an evidence technician hurry by with an ivory-handled knife sealed in a plastic bag.

The murder weapon?

Remembering the dull glint of light on metal, Sydney flinched. An unwelcome empathy subjected her to the feel of slicing pain as the blade plunged through skin, glancing off bone and severing veins or arteries with each thrust. She could feel hot blood welling up through the wounds, and feel, too, the icy fingers of shock tighten its grip on her heart . . .

She sat up abruptly. It wasn't helping matters to let her imagination run wild.

She thought about the phone again, wondering what her chances were at finding one and making a call without being detected. Dwight Grant wouldn't be pleased to find that she'd disregarded his order to stay, but she'd been held incommunicado for—

Again the door opened, and this time a uniformed deputy stepped inside. "Miss Bryant?" At her nod, he continued, "I'm supposed to escort you down to the department so you can give your statement."

"Then will I be allowed to go?"

The deputy shrugged, using his thumb to flick a breath mint into his mouth. "If I could tell the future," he said around the mint, "I'd be on Donahue, instead of pulling a graveyard shift. Come on."

They saw no one on the way out, but overhead a helicopter was shining a wide beam of light on the bushes as a foot patrol combed the grounds with dogs.

Chapter Eleven

Wednesday

Shortly before three a.m., Sydney signed a statement typed by a scowling deputy who'd utilized a two-fingered hunt-and-peck system on an old Royal manual that gave new meaning to the word portable.

Like a bad penny, Lieutenant Dwight Grant showed up just as she crossed the 't' in Bryant and snatched the sheets of paper from under her hand.

"You know this—" he waved the statement at her "—marks the end of your *case,* don't you?"

She nodded, in truth not at all displeased. Her psyche was badly bruised from the trauma of finding Martina Saxon's body, and to make matters worse, she would have to deal with the guilt of knowing that the murder had been committed practically under her nose.

The sooner she was off the case the better. All that remained to hold her was Victor . . .

Victor. With everything that had happened, she hadn't given him a thought until now. As much as she dreaded it, she should be the one to tell him . . . but was there a way to break the news gently? Could she find the words that would soften the blow?

"—for comparison," Grant was saying. "I know the DOJ has them on file from your investigator's license application but it would speed things up considerably if we took them again now."

Her mind on other things, it took her a second to realize Grant was asking her to be fingerprinted. "Whatever you want," she said, and thought, *anything to get out of here.*

A furry caterpillar of an eyebrow lifted in mock surprise. "Good."

He tucked her statement into the manila folder he was carrying, and she saw that she had not been the only one brought to the station; there were at least four statements in the folder in addition to her own. She caught just a glimpse of the others, but was able to make out Owen Saxon's name on one.

"I'll walk you down," Grant said, taking her firmly by the elbow, and ushering her out of the cubbyhole office into the hall which was swarming with activity despite the lateness of the hour.

The death of an heiress accounted for that.

Minutes later, as she wiped the black ink off her fingertips, Grant crossed to the door and held it open. "Thanks for your cooperation, Miss Bryant," he said without an ounce of sincerity. "Be sure to drive safely on your way home.

The welcome mat—threadbare as it was—had been withdrawn.

The air was heavy with fog and she had to use windshield wipers to see. Their rhythm threatened to lull her to sleep and she cracked the window, letting the cool moist air revive her.

After a couple of miscues onto residential streets, she got her bearings and made her way to Interstate 5, heading south toward the city. There was light traffic on the freeway, most of it headed north toward Orange County or beyond to Los Angeles, and for a change the drivers were driving slow, respectful of the limited visibility.

Isolated by the fog, which varied in consistency from being as thick as cotton candy to ghostly wisps that trailed across the road, she settled in, resting her head against the tall back of the seat as she drove. The freeway skirted the coastline, and the briny smell of rotted seaweed made her wrinkle her nose with distaste. When the smell thickened and intensified, she gave up and pressed the control to close the window tight; the cool air was bracing, but she'd stay awake some other way.

One other way was replaying the snippets of conversation she'd overheard at the sheriff's sub-station back in her mind:

". . . no signs of forced entry . . ."

". . . a body found in water isn't going to present much in the way of physical evidence . . ."

". . . can't recall when they saw her last . . ."

". . . wasn't a kitchen knife. The killer brought it for that purpose . . ."

". . . penetrated the aorta, so it would've been quick, if not painless . . ."

". . . didn't hear a scream . . ."

Sydney felt the weariness sink into her bones, taking root in the marrow. All at once she felt depleted, void of energy. She thought of home—of a hot shower and the comfort of her bed—and it took the last of her willpower to keep from calling it a night.

"Victor," she said, "where am I going to find you?"

Sydney made the circuit of several of Victor's favorite hangouts—a twenty-four hour donut shop on Balboa, the taco stand where she'd

74

found him on Monday night, the Denny's on Miramar Road, and an all-night market that served exotic blends of fresh ground coffee to insomniatic shoppers—before hitting on the right one: a scruffy little bar in Pacific Beach.

The Fried Clam filled the dry hours between two and six a.m. by metamorphosing into a game room of sorts. Patrons could select one of dozens of games, including old board standbys like Monopoly, Parcheesi, Clue, or Jeopardy, as well as more recent pretenders, such as Trivial Pursuit.

There were dart boards, checker boards, and chess sets, and a box full of decks of cards. Gambling on the outcome of any game was officially prohibited—or so a neatly lettered sign on the wall read—but the management turned a blind eye to the cash changing hands.

Depending on how sociable one felt, there were team games and tournaments at one extreme, and at the other, the ever popular Solitaire.

Victor Griffith was playing Solitaire. Or at least he had the cards spread out in front of him. Both elbows were propped on the table, his hands clenched in fists holding up his head while covering his eyes.

Sydney hesitated; she could almost see the waves of misery radiating from him.

He'd heard.

Of course, he'd heard. Victor was the very essence of a journalist, whose thirst for news could never be quenched. His heart beat to the pulse of the presses, and printer's ink flowed in his veins.

He would have heard a cryptic word or two over the police scanner in his van, caught the code for homicide, recognized the urgency in some cop's voice. And he would have immediately started making calls, tapping sources, probing to uncover whatever he could.

Like Pandora's Box, once open, there was no way that he could close the lid he'd pried off, no way to harness the demons he'd unknowingly set loose . . . no way to *not* know about Martina.

From somewhere deep inside, Sydney found the resolve to step forward. She sat beside Victor and placed a hand on his forearm. A tremor passed through him, and she felt the muscle contract violently beneath her touch.

"Victor, it's Sydney."

His fingers clenched even more, skin whitening over bony knuckles that looked as though they might split through his flesh. He ground those knuckles into his eyes, perhaps trying to keep the tears back.

"Victor," she said again, more softly. She watched a tear drop from his little finger onto the jack of diamonds, saw his prominent Ad-am's apple bob as he swallowed repeatedly as he worked to hold his feelings in.

She squeezed his arm, then stroked it, acutely aware of the coiled fury of muscle and tendon, a fury barely contained. Across the room, someone laughed.

"I'm so sorry." Her fingers encircled Victor's left wrist, and she pulled gently, wanting—no, needing—to look into his eyes, to gauge whether or not it would be safe to leave him alone to his sorrow . . .

He allowed her to bring first his left and then his right hand down, but kept his eyes closed. His face looked more gaunt than usual, his cheeks hollower, as though he'd taken suddenly ill.

Which, she supposed, he had. Heartsick, her mother would say.

"Look at me," she implored.

He shook his head. "Can't."

Even speaking a single word, his voice sounded raw with grief. If she'd had any doubts lingering over the depth of his love for Martina Saxon, they were swept away by the agony reverberating in that one word.

Holding his left hand in both of hers, Sydney fell silent. She owed it to him to tell him about her part in the discovery of Martina's body—she didn't want him to hear *that* from another source—but now wasn't the time.

For now, all she could do was sit with him so he wouldn't be alone when daylight came and made his nightmare real.

Chapter Twelve

Sydney adjusted the shower spray to fine and increased the flow, letting the water sting her in a thousand tiny needle points. As numb as she still felt, it took as much to have any effect at all.

That was what came of having a breakfast glass of white wine. As a chaser for exhaustion, wine left a lot to be desired.

At six a.m., The Fried Clam had resumed serving drinks, and Victor had gotten rip-roaring drunk in record time, slamming back tequila shooters until he was salting the table instead of the back of his hand. At his insistence, and as part of a negotiated agreement to leave, she'd been talked into accepting six ounces of the house chablis.

The house in question favored jug wines with screw-top caps. Such were the hazards of negotiating without giving thought to the consequences.

After she'd delivered Victor back to his apartment and seen him off to bed, she'd come home, intending to do the same for herself. But despite a slight buzz from the wine—which usually would have knocked her for a loop—an hour of tossing and turning had been enough to convince her that sleep was just not happening . . .

There were few things as tiring as trying to force sleep.

She lifted her face to the spray, hoping the hot water might sweat the alcohol from her pores. Pinpricks of water pelted her eyelids, and she opened her mouth, grateful for the opportunity to rinse the wine's aftertaste from her tongue.

She stayed in the shower longer than she should have, trying to warm the chill that had settled inside her, but succeeded only in making her body feel limp. It crossed her mind that as languid as she felt, she ought to give going to bed another shot, but somehow it had gotten to be noon, and there were other things to do.

Sydney had just inserted the key into the deadbolt of her office door when she heard footsteps.

There was a reasonable amount of traffic among the offices that shared the second floor, and thus not unusual for someone to come up behind her, but between anonymous phone calls, vandalism, and murder, her nerves were a trifle edgy, and she whirled.

Whirled, and came face to face with Boyd Harrington, the Saxon family attorney. Impeccably attired in a gray pinstriped suit, white on white shirt, and lemon yellow tie, he exuded affluence and influence in equal measures.

"Miss Bryant?" he asked calmly, his composure not the least bit disturbed.

Sydney brushed her hair, still damp from the shower, out of her face. "Mr. Harrington, what a surprise."

"Oh," he said, his chiseled features assuming a less formal expression, "have we met? I shouldn't admit that I don't recall being introduced to as striking a young lady as you are, but—" he smiled and shook his head with regret "—I am a married man."

"We haven't met, Mr. Harrington, but of course I know who you are."

"Really?" He tapped his temple with a manicured finger. "Well, at least I'm not going senile, forgetting a face like yours."

"Far from it." Harrington was as wily as a fox and twice as quick, but if he intended to lay the charm on any thicker, he'd be needing a trowel. "What brings you here, Mr. Harrington?"

He reached and took the keys from her hand, unerringly choosing the correct one to unlock the door, and then doing so. "An excellent question, right to the point. Shall we go inside and talk?"

"All right." She retrieved her keys from him— his hands were softer than hers—and walked past him, and as she did, she caught a scent of perfume. His wife's? Somehow the musky fragrance didn't match the aging blonde she'd seen with him last night.

She remembered then that last night he'd been holding a handkerchief to his face, and she glanced over her shoulder at him to see if she could find the cause.

Something in Harrington's eyes changed and the smile he gave her was curiously intimate.

Had he misinterpreted her glance as flirtatiousness? If so, he couldn't be more wrong. There was no denying that he was an attractive man, but she had a strong sense that beneath the superficial charm and courtliness beat a heart as cold as dry ice.

Still, she studied his face, willing to chance inviting his attentions for a closer look. The lighting wasn't great—the venetian blinds were shut—but there along the right side of his face was a scratch, origin unknown.

It was barely noticeable, perhaps an inch and a half to two inches long, and remarkably straight. The edges were slightly reddened, but there wasn't a scab.

Interesting, she thought. Her mind ran through a short list of causal agents—a straight pin left in the collar of a new shirt, a wicked nick from an old-fashioned straight-edge razor, or an unseen branch swinging back and catching him unprepared—before settling on the most obvious: a woman's fingernails being raked down his face.

Sydney tossed the keys on her desk and turned on the light, then went to the window to open the blinds. She wanted a better look at him.

"Very nice," Harrington said, eyes sweeping around the room, missing nothing. "Business is good?"

"I guess I can't complain." She didn't believe for a second that he was favorably impressed by what he saw; she'd been in his offices once, serving a summons to one of his junior associates who was the respondent in a divorce case, and had waded through carpet deep enough to lose a Shetland pony in.

"Glad to hear it." He sat opposite the desk. "Now it's my turn to come right to the point, Miss Bryant," he said, and then didn't, instead smiling as he adjusted the crease in his pant leg.

Sydney sat down and waited. She was in no hurry; in this light it looked as if he had tried to cover the scratch on his face with make-up, a shade paler than his own skin. Trying to hide it, she supposed, but from whose eyes?

"I understand from the police that you were the one who called them."

"Yes, that's right."

"And you were on the property ... private property ... prior to the discovery of the—" he hesitated, closed his eyes, and swallowed hard. Then he held up a hand as if to forestall an interruption, and said, "Martina."

The last was hushed, almost a whisper, and she wondered at Harrington's show of emotion. True, he was a corporate lawyer, not as familiar with death as a criminal lawyer would be, but she did not find his demeanor credible. He couldn't have survived and flourished as he had in the jungle warfare of corporate law with the Tootsie Roll Pop soft center he was affecting.

"I was there," she said, matter-of-factly adding, "and I found the body, as I'm sure you know."

The line of his jaw tightened; clearly he had scripted this encounter, and she wasn't adhering to his scenario. "I do indeed know."

"Then why don't you ask me whatever it is you came here to ask me, and save us both some time?"

The man had an entire repertoire of smiles; this one didn't reach his eyes. "For reasons known only to herself—and I should add, against my counsel—Mrs. Saxon has requested that I bring you to Villa Saxon to talk to her."

It was not what she expected, and it threw her for a moment. "Martina's mother?"

"Grandmother. She would have come to your office—" he had the grace not to shudder "—but she's not feeling well this morning, as I'm sure you can understand."

He'd left out the 'even' before 'you.' Sydney felt a grudging admiration for his restraint.

Harrington stood. "She sent her car for your convenience. Of course, she doesn't wish to disrupt your schedule, but if you can spare an hour?"

It sounded so very considerate, but Sydney knew without question that Miss Penelope wasn't one for issuing requests. This was a command performance.

There'd been a dozen messages on her answering machine at home and the call indicator light was blinking furiously on the office machine. Mitch had called, and so had Ethan's secretary, Valentine Lund.

Besides, she should dictate a verbal version of the statement she'd given the police while events were still fresh in her mind. She also wanted to type up a report for the case file, despite Victor's insistence that he could never stand to read it. And she was beginning to get a headache from either the wine or the lack of sleep, or a combination thereof.

But the work could wait, and as for the headache . . .

"Would you happen to have an aspirin on you?" she asked as she stood up and reached for her keys.

Chapter Thirteen

Boyd Harrington extended a hand to help her out of the limousine, his expression one of thinly veiled disdain.

Sydney wondered about that. Had he decided she did not merit his concern? Because she was certain that he *had* been concerned over bringing her to see Penelope Day Saxon, although she couldn't fathom why.

"This way, Miss Bryant," Harrington said, his tone once again formal, his pronunciation crisp and precise.

That precision probably endeared him to court stenographers, and maybe she was just feeling testy, but he was beginning to get to her. The man was mercurial to a fault, with his hot and cold running attitudes. Then again, she'd often thought that — with the exception of Ethan — lawyers were little more than actors whose performances were given before an audience of twelve.

In Harrington's case, with his imperial manner, it was easy to imagine him in a powdered wig, pleading his case in an English courtroom.

"Yes, sire," she said, and couldn't stop herself from curtseying, a skill she'd acquired as a child and hadn't used since. It wasn't as easy as she recalled, but then, her center of gravity had been a lot closer to the ground when she was six.

The chauffeur, who had opened the limo door and was standing nearby, cracked a grin which he covered by coughing into his gloved hand.

Harrington glowered at her. "You will remember, Miss Bryant, that this is a house of bereavement."

Wavering between contrition and defiance, she said nothing, but walked past him, toward the front door of the house. As she approached, memories of the night before returned in full force.

This is a house of death, a voice in her mind amended.

Harrington was following close behind her, and only his presence there kept her from stopping cold. When they reached the door, he pressed the bell impatiently, several times in rapid succession.

A moment later the door opened, and Sydney recognized the woman standing at the threshold as having been the driver of the Volvo last night. Daylight made her features appear even more severe. Hers wasn't a mouth accustomed to smiling, Sydney thought.

"Edith," Harrington said, "would you kindly inform Miss Penelope that we're here?"

The woman's slate gray eyes narrowed, but she inclined her head as she stepped aside, letting them enter the foyer. "Right away, Mr. Harrington," she said as she closed the door behind them.

Sydney watched after the woman as she went to perform her duty. Had the police happened across the note Sydney had seen her toss from the car window? If not, maybe she could find it.

Later, she thought. For now she was intrigued by how quickly the foyer had been restored to order; last night on her way out, she noticed the tell-tale residue of fingerprint powder on virtually every surface in the room. Now there wasn't a trace left . . .

Harrington put his hand on the small of her back and guided her to the left, toward the door that last night had seemed to shelter darkness.

"We'll wait in the library," he said.

The library was one of the few that Sydney had seen in a private residence that warranted the name. All four walls were lined from floor to ceiling with bookshelves. The shelves were crammed with books, books whose cracked spines revealed they weren't merely for show. There were books as well stacked several feet high on the round oak table in the center of the room.

There were reading chairs in each corner, marvelous chairs, thick-cushioned and perfect for reading on a rainy afternoon. Floorlamps beside each provided adequate light. Sydney felt a pang of envy for whoever might while away the hours lost in the magic of a book, curled up in one of those chairs.

Looking farther, she noticed that the room had no windows, which explained the utter blackness of the night before.

Harrington glanced at his Rolex, frowned, and went to stand in front of a row of encyclopedias, one of several sets on the shelves. He absently ran a finger along the scratch on his face.

Sydney realized that he was deliberately ignoring her. No more Mr. Nice Guy, she thought.

Penelope Day Saxon knew how to enter a

room. Slender and petite at less than five feet tall, her bearing was that of a woman half her age, her shoulders straight and squared, and her gait showed none of the hesitancy that her years might justify. She was dressed in funereal black — a stark contrast to her silver hair — wearing a calf-length silk dress that drew attention to her still shapely ankles.

As a young girl, Penelope Day had been a beauty, and a lifetime of wealth and privilege had preserved that beauty, even enhanced it. Youth was no match for self-confident maturity.

Age had caught up to her only in her parchment-fine skin, and in the network of thin blue veins that showed beneath. Grief had marked her less obviously, in a slight puffiness below red-rimmed eyes.

"You must be Sydney Bryant," she said, offering her hand.

Sydney took it gently; the bones felt as fragile as a hummingbird's. "I am. I'm pleased to meet you, even if this isn't . . . the best of times."

"It isn't," Miss Penelope agreed. "Thank you for coming to see me."

"It's the least I can do," Sydney said. "I am sorry for your loss."

"Thank you dear." Her gaze went to Harrington, and she gave a slight nod. Then she crossed to the nearest of the high-backed chairs and sat down, folding her hands primly in her lap.

"Miss Bryant," the lawyer said, taking his cue, "the police have informed us that you were hired by a male co-worker of Martina's to investigate her relationships with other men. Is that correct?"

"Essentially, yes."

"You undertook this . . . investigation . . . on Monday of this week?"

"That's also correct."

"I assume you won't mind sharing with us what you found out."

Miss Penelope raised one hand off her lap, turning palm up as if in genteel supplication.

Sydney could find no harm in complying, so she related as succinctly as possible what she'd done and learned in the day and a half she'd worked the case. As an afterthought, she recited the names—or those that she could remember—of the young men Martina had dated, watching Harrington blink after each name as though he were checking them off some mental list.

"And your efforts on your client's behalf resulted in your presence on the grounds last night," Harrington mused when she'd finished.

"Yes."

"But I don't understand why you felt the need, given that you'd already collected more than enough information on Martina and her . . . acquaintances?"

Sydney frowned. "A lot of what I do is . . . is distant or removed from the people involved. I can tap into all kinds of records and information by computer, make a few calls and get even more."

"Computers," Miss Penelope said, sounding vaguely distressed, as though it hadn't occurred to her that technology would dare intrude on her privacy or that of her family.

"I've had cases," Sydney continued, "that I could have brought to a satisfactory conclusion without ever setting foot outside my office door. But I never feel like I've done my job unless I relate to the—" her mind searched for an acceptable alternative to 'subject' and came up empty "—to my subject on a different level."

"What you mean is, until you've finished invading their privacy."

She added hypocrite to her profile of Harrington. Part of a lawyer's stock-in-trade was uncovering the dirty little secrets of an adversary. He damned well knew that there was no such thing as absolute privacy these days, and no doubt had profited from the knowledge gained by violating a foe's secrecy.

Sydney continued as if he hadn't spoken: "A personal level. I wanted to see Martina with a date. I thought after that, I'd be better able to advise my client. . . ."

"I have some advice for your client," Harrington said with a frown.

His was rather more than the professional outrage Sydney would have expected. Had there been something between him and Martina?

"I advise him to—"

Miss Penelope sat forward. "Excuse me for interrupting, Boyd, but this isn't the purpose of this meeting."

She'd spoken softly, without raising her voice, but it was enough: Harrington's mouth snapped shut with tooth-jarring force.

"Miss Bryant, or may I call you Sydney?"

"Please do."

"Sydney." She gave a little nod. "I will admit to being as curious as Boyd is about the specifics of your investigation, but that isn't really what I wanted to speak to you about."

Sydney glanced at the lawyer. "No?"

"Not at all. What I would like, Sydney dear, is for you to work for me."

For several seconds she drew a blank, as though the synapses in her brain had short-circuited, depriving her of rational thought. She almost laughed—it was that unexpected—but Miss Penelope's expression was serious.

"I would like you to find out who killed my

94

granddaughter."

"But . . . but . . ."

Harrington's lock-jaw was cured. "This is a matter for the police," he said. It had the sound of an oft-repeated argument.

"I will, of course, inform the authorities," Miss Penelope continued, casting a cool glance in his direction, "that you're to have their complete and unequivocal cooperation."

Sydney shook her head, confused. "I have to agree with Mr. Harrington; murder is most definitely a matter for the police. California law is specific—"

"Of course it is, I'm not denying that, and I'm quite familiar with the law on that point. They will proceed with their investigation—even I can't stop them from that—in their bureaucratic way. But I want you to conduct a second investigation, a *personal* investigation, reporting to me. And only to me."

"This is insane," Harrington muttered.

"I'm entitled to a moment of insanity," Miss Penelope said, her tone sharper. "Humor an old woman who's lost a favorite grandchild."

Sydney thought she'd never seen anyone who looked less like an old woman . . . or more sane. "But why me?"

"Why not you?"

"Well, I . . ."

"You strike me as being a perceptive, bright young woman. It's evident that you are efficient and thorough in the work you do, and my sources—" she glanced sideways at Harrington "—inform me that you're well-regarded in your field."

"That's all very well, but—"

"But nothing." Miss Penelope rose from the chair. "Boyd will tell you that I'm used to having my way. I've no idea why he's bothering to argue with me, unless he's gotten it into his head that he has to protect me, as he has done for the last fifteen years."

Harrington said nothing.

"However," she went on, "I don't believe that I have anything to fear from learning the truth."

Famous last words; Sydney had seen clients hurt, even devastated, from learning the truth. Particularly in a case like this . . .

"In a case like this," Harrington said, eerily echoing her thoughts, "where most of the suspects are family—"

"That doesn't make any difference."

Harrington looked genuinely saddened. "You know better."

"I will thank you not to tell me what I know." Miss Penelope turned her gaze to Sydney. "The police have suggested that there may not have been an intruder, as they first suspected."

Sydney had anticipated that the police would reach that conclusion, but it seemed odd to her that they'd told Miss Penelope of their suspicions. Obviously the Saxon family had friends in very high places . . .

"But I don't want to prejudice your investigation by saying any more." Miss Penelope smiled. "You will take the case, won't you?"

Sydney hesitated only briefly. "Yes, I believe I will."

Chapter Fourteen

A moment after she closed the door to the library, Sydney's pager went off — a weak battery made it sound like someone was strangling a canary — and she stopped to look at the number on the display.

Boyd Harrington's voice carried clearly through the door. "I have to warn you . . . the day may come when you regret this, Penelope."

"Ah, yes, a lawyer's creed: Never ask a question you don't already know the answer to."

"Or that you don't *want* to know the answer to."

"Want to or not, I have to know."

From the corner of her eye, Sydney detected movement, and she turned to see the housekeeper standing in the doorway that led to the courtyard. The mud brown color of her dress blended in with the background well enough that if she hadn't moved, Sydney might not have known she was there.

"Easy, isn't it?" the woman said. "They think

no one would be so ill-mannered as to listen in."

In spite of the fact that it hadn't been her intention to eavesdrop, Sydney felt herself begin to blush. She moved guiltily away from the door. "Is there a phone I can use? I've got a call."

"Of course. This way."

Sydney followed the housekeeper into the living room, and as they passed through, she noticed that here, too, all signs of police activity had been eliminated. The glass decanter and brandy snifters were gone, and even the ashes in the fireplace had been swept away.

The housekeeper reached the hallway that had been backlit last night and turned left. They walked past several other doorways, some of which were open, including one bright sunny room where she saw a blue Princess-style telephone on a desk.

"Excuse me," Sydney said. "Edith, isn't it?"

"It is," the woman answered but didn't stop. "Edith Armstrong. Used to be Edmonds."

"Mrs. Armstrong—"

"Tut! Call me Edith; living here has cured me of putting on airs."

"Edith, where are we going?"

"To the kitchen, Miss Bryant, so that you can use the phone."

"But—"

"That one doesn't work. Hasn't worked in

years. Miss Penelope is something of a collector of times past. Old phones, old radios and the like."

Making conversation, Sydney said, "That's an interesting hobby."

"You wouldn't think so if you had to dust 'em. Has a warehouse in Orange County full of old cars. At least those I don't have to dust."

They had reached the end of the hall, which in this direction terminated at double swinging doors. The housekeeper pushed the right door open, standing aside as Sydney went through.

As kitchens went, this one looked mildly dangerous. The huge commercial side-by-side refrigerator/freezer, Jenn-Air oven and stove, microwave, trash compactor, and dishwasher were all black, and pretty much everything else was stainless steel or glass.

Gleaming copper pots and pans hung from a silver rack over the cooking island in the center of the room. Rows of rosewood-handled knives and cooking utensils were lined at exact intervals along a magnetic strip on the wall above the sink.

Behind glass cabinet doors were the finest Limoges porcelain—what appeared to be a modest service for sixty—and crystal so delicate that she thought it might chip from a hard look.

"Help yourself," the housekeeper said, gesturing toward a white wallphone and then leaning against a spotless counter with her arms folded across her chest.

"Thank you." Sydney picked up the receiver and quickly pressed the keypads from memory, listening to a familiar touch-tone song. The line—Mitch's private number—was busy. She depressed the switchhook and was preparing to try a second time when the housekeeper spoke.

"I understand you're going to investigate Martina's death."

Sydney replaced the receiver and turned. "That's right. You overheard?"

"Just now? No, I was checking to make sure the maids had put fresh towels in the dressing rooms, though I suppose it might be a while before any of them take a mind to go into the pool."

Sydney couldn't swear to it, because the woman remained expressionless, but she thought that Edith was amused. "Then—"

"Mr. Harrington was here earlier this morning. He has a mouth on him, that one does."

"I can imagine." Sydney hesitated, trying to read the signals Edith Armstrong was sending. It seemed obvious that she wanted to talk, and no doubt had an agenda to fulfill—as everyone did—but Sydney had a sense that there might be more to it than that.

"He was hoping," the housekeeper went on, "that you'd turn Miss Penelope down."

Not exactly an earth-shattering revelation, but

interesting. "Wouldn't she have just gone out and hired someone else?"

"Ah, but then she'd most likely hire an investigator he recommended."

"What's wrong with that?"

Edith Armstrong bent forward slightly from the waist, lowering her voice to a whisper. "He'd only recommend someone he could *control.*"

Sydney asked the obvious question: "Why does Harrington need control?"

"And there you have it," was her ambiguous reply. She tilted her head a shade to the left and then moved suddenly away from the counter, grabbing a tea kettle off the stove and hurrying to the sink to fill it.

"Edith," she said as the kitchen door swung open and Boyd Harrington came in.

Sydney jumped; she hadn't heard him coming. But Edith obviously had.

His eyes darted from Sydney to the housekeeper and back again. "I wondered where you'd wandered off to. I'm due back at my office in thirty minutes." He tapped the face of his Rolex. "I assume you're ready to go."

"Actually, I—"

"Good." He took two steps closer to Edith, who had turned off the faucet and was carefully wiping drops of water off the outside of the kettle with a dish towel. "Tea is late, Edith."

"I'm sorry, sir."

"You know she isn't well."

Edith looked affronted. "If anyone knows how Miss Penelope is feeling, I do. I've worked in this house, for this family—"

"Edith, please." Harrington sounded tired. "Just prepare the afternoon tea and see to it that she takes a rest afterward. All right?"

"I will."

There still was no expression on the house-keeper's face, but Sydney would have bet the farm that an unspoken 'you son of a bitch' was echoing in the woman's head.

Harrington turned his attention once again to her. "Shall we go?"

Outside, Harrington walked past the limousine toward his Jaguar, which was parked along the inside of the circular drive. He'd unlocked the passenger door and opened it before he realized that she was not following at his heels like some obedient little puppy.

Sydney rested her elbows on the limo's roof, smiling when he turned to look for her.

"Miss Bryant, didn't I say that I have to be in town in thirty, no make that—" he consulted his watch "—twenty-four minutes now?"

She nodded, still smiling.

"You heard that, did you? Well then, what *is* the problem?"

"There's no problem."

"No problem? Perhaps you have a short attention span, then, because—"

"I didn't realize that you were intending to drive your own car," she said.

"Oh? Have something against Jags, do you?"

"Not at all."

"Don't trust me behind the wheel?"

Sydney had seldom heard a more leading question, but she let it pass. "If it's all the same to you, I'd prefer to let the chauffeur take me back to my office."

"The chauffeur."

"Yes. That way I can start my investigation now instead of later."

For a moment, Harrington stood motionless. Then he slammed the passenger door—the Jag absorbed this abuse solidly—and stormed around the front of the car to the driver's side. He tried to yank that door open, but it was locked. The delay in opening the door upset his momentum and robbed his tantrum of impact.

Unseemly behavior from a man with his professional standing.

"Good afternoon, Mr. Harrington," she called to him as he was about to get into the car.

He glared at her. "I intend to keep an eye on you, Miss Bryant."

"I wouldn't have it any other way."

His tires flung a little gravel when he pulled away a few seconds later.

* * *

Sydney went looking for Edith Armstrong, hoping to finish their conversation. But although only a few minutes had passed since she'd left the housekeeper in the kitchen, when she returned the room was empty.

Serving tea to Miss Penelope, she thought. How long would that take?

While she was waiting, she decided to try again to return Mitch's call. She had gotten through the three-digit prefix when the door whooshed open behind her.

"Shit," she swore under her breath, and thought, *caught off-guard again*. She hung up the phone and turned, but it wasn't the housekeeper standing there.

Owen Saxon frowned at her. "Who the hell are you?"

Chapter Fifteen

Owen Saxon was one of those young men who could almost be called pretty. He shared his sister's fair coloring and was blessed with the classic features of an Adonis. His eyes were a vivid blue, with long dark eyelashes beneath finely-arched brows.

All that spoiled his looks was the petulant set of his mouth. His full lower lip seemed designed solely to pout . . .

Some women would find that attractive, Sydney knew, and was thankful she wasn't one of them.

"I said, who the hell are you?" he repeated.

She glanced down, waiting for him to stamp his foot. When he didn't, she met his eyes. "My name is Sydney Bryant and I'm a private investigator. Your grandmother has hired me to look into Martina's death."

Beneath his tan, he paled.

"I understand that her death must have come as a shock to you—"

"My God, yes."

106

"—but would you mind answering a few questions?"

He held up a hand palm outward, as if to ward her off. "I don't know anything about it."

"Now that's an interesting point. Most of the people I've interviewed over the years felt that they had little or no information to offer. But it's surprising, sometimes, what they know."

"Not this time," Owen Saxon said, shaking his head vehemently.

"The oddest things, things that on the surface appear to have no possible relevance, often turn out to be significant."

"I don't know *any*thing."

Sydney regarded him for a moment, noticing that he'd clenched his hands into fists. His body seemed rigid with tension to the extent that the muscles in his neck were corded, the veins distended.

"Have you spoken with the police?" she asked, trying a different tactic.

His eyes widened slightly. "No, I haven't."

That was an out and out lie; she'd seen his name on a statement last night. Strange that he would lie about something that she could easily disprove.

"Why should I talk to the police?" he went on. "I told you and I'd tell them—"

"You don't know anything," she finished for him. "But I'm sure they're going to want to talk to you, regardless. They're very thorough. Persistent. Even relentless. And when you *do* talk to them, well . . . be careful."

It was more or less a bluff, but he fell for it; at twenty-four, he was basically an overgrown child.

"Be careful about what?"

She used one of Harrington's tricks and made a show of looking at her watch. "Be careful or you might be sorry. Listen, I've got to go . . ."

"Wait a minute," Owen Saxon said, grabbing her arm as she walked by. "Why should I be sorry? I haven't done anything."

"I'm sure you haven't."

"And I don't know anything about Martina's murder. I didn't even get home till five this morning."

She peeled his fingers from around her arm. "But you were probably here when she was killed, Owen."

"What? No, that's not possible."

"It is possible. When was the last time you saw Martina alive?"

He stammered for a few seconds before getting the words out: "At dinner. All of us had an early dinner together, around five-thirty or six."

"How did Martina seem to you?"

He shrugged, reached up and stroked his own hair. "I don't know. Normal, I guess. I wasn't paying much attention to her."

Hearing an undercurrent of anger in his voice and remembering the look on his face when he'd driven by in his Ferrari last night, she asked: "Who *were* you paying attention to?"

"My brother David." His smile lasted a fraction of a second. "Big brother David, mankind's last shining hope for the future."

"Did you have an argument?"

"A discussion. We had a discussion."

"About what?"

The petulant cast to his face hardened into bitterness. "Father has been playing favorites again; he named David to a vice presidency at Saxon and Associates."

"And you felt the position should be yours?"

"Heaven forbid. I'm not the corporate type."

Sydney frowned. "Then what was the problem?"

"The problem is David. He thinks by working in one of the family businesses, he can improve on his first-born status, and squeeze me out."

"Why would he want to do that?"

"Ask him why. Maybe he doesn't think a third of my parents' estate will be enough for him and Miss Congeniality to get by on."

The conversation had taken a detour from Martina, but Sydney had a suspicion that the key to Owen Saxon could be found by listening to his complaints. She did her best at looking sympathetic, nodding as if in agreement to encourage him to continue.

Which he did.

"It won't do him any good, though." Smugness fit him like a second skin. "The trust is irrevocable. I had an attorney look at it."

An attorney, she thought. Not Harrington?

"When the day comes, dear David will find that all of his manipulation has been for nothing. He'll get a third and not a dime more."

"Don't you mean half?"

"What?"

The accentuation of the last consonant was such that Sydney almost expected the delicate crystal to shatter behind the glass cabinet doors. "Half. Now that Martina is . . . has been killed, won't you and your brother split the estate evenly?"

He did not answer, but given the wariness in his eyes, she interpreted his silence as instinctive self-preservation. Despite all the talk of thirds, he'd long since tallied up his sister's death on the family ledger, and found himself in line for a tidy little profit. Pretending that the financial consequences of murder hadn't crossed his mind was merely another form of camouflage.

Sydney kept her voice neutral. "That's right, isn't it?"

"I suppose it is."

Gambling that now he'd be preoccupied with putting verbal distance between himself and a show of avarice, she changed gears. "So during your discussion with David, Martina didn't take sides?"

He blinked. "No. She never took sides over

110

petty things like money. Besides, all she cared about lately was her job."

"I understand that she was an intern at the *Union*."

"If you say so. She acted like she was with the CIA, always asking questions—"

"Questions about what?"

"Whatever. You name it. A few weeks ago, I had my car in for service, and when I mentioned it to her, she all but interrogated me. Did I see the part they'd removed from the engine, had they given me a written estimate, that kind of thing."

Sydney wasn't sure what to make of that, if anything. Maybe Martina's enthusiasm for investigative reporting—thwarted at the *Union,* where she was primarily a gofer in the library—had found an outlet at home.

Could that enthusiasm, which prompted her to see a snake under every rock, have driven her to turn over one too many rocks?

You're getting ahead of yourself, she thought. First things first.

"What did you do after dinner?" she asked.

"I took a quick shower and got dressed. Then I left, and went straight to The Tides."

"Where's your room in relation to Martina's?"

"Across the hall. But I already told you, I didn't see her after dinner, I—"

"Who left the table first?"

"I did, I think." He pulled at his right earlobe, his eye movement rapid as he considered it. "Yes, definitely, I got up before she did. She was twirling her wine glass, the way women do."

"So you may have been in the shower when she went to her room to get ready for the evening."

"That's probably right."

"When you left your room later, did you hear any sounds coming from her room?"

"If I did, I can't remember."

"And where is your room relative to the pool?"

"My room?"

Sydney nodded. "Did you walk by the pool on your way out?"

"No, I went the other way. This place, if you haven't noticed, is a big square with a courtyard in the middle. The inside rooms open into the courtyard, the outside rooms overlook the grounds. There's a hallway in between. To get to the front of the house, you can either cut through the courtyard or walk the long way through the hall."

"And you took the long way." At his nod, she asked, "Was there a reason for that?"

"I didn't want to run into my brother," he said, and looked away, avoiding her eyes.

"Your discussion was that heated?"

Owen Saxon sighed. "As Grandmother would say, it was spirited."

112

"Did you see anyone on your way out?"

"In the hall? No. But when I got to the living room, I saw Julie Harrington. And my father and mother were there, ready to leave. They asked me if I wanted to ride with them, but I had plans for after the Festival."

"Anyone else?"

"Edith, of course."

At that, the kitchen door swung open, and the housekeeper, who most likely had been listening to all of it, came in with a china tea service on a silver tray.

"Owen," she said, "your mother has been looking for you. The tailor is here to fit your suit for the funeral."

Chapter Sixteen

Sydney had wanted to take a look around Villa Saxon to get her bearings straight, but it seemed inappropriate to her to do so while the family was preparing their mourning attire.

She found the chauffeur polishing the hubcaps of the limousine and a minute later, they were off. They had reached the crest of the hill when she remembered the note that Edith Armstrong had tossed out the window the night before.

There was an intercom between the driver and passenger sections, and she pressed the transmit button.

"Yes miss."

"Would you stop for a moment, please?"

"Here?"

"Please."

The Benz pulled to the right side of the road and came smoothly to a stop. "Is there something wrong?" the chauffeur asked.

"Not at all." She studied the array of controls

in the door panel, took a chance and was right: the lock disengaged with a subtle click. "Just something I want to have a look at. It won't take long."

She got out of the limo and hurried down the hill as quickly as her footing on the gravel would allow. Glancing at the willow under whose sheltering branches she'd hidden, she tried to estimate where the housekeeper's Volvo had been when the note was tossed out.

She doubted that the crumpled paper would have gone far initially, but it might have been blown farther since. The bushes here were well-tended, and there was clearance between the bottom of the shrubbery and the ground.

Propelled by currents of air from passing cars—and there'd been a lot of them in the last eighteen hours—there was no telling where the note might have wound up. Except . . . except there was a single set of footprints in the soft dirt on the side of the road.

The prints were those of a man and they tracked from the gravel road to a point approximately six feet in. There, the footprints did an about-face, returning with an occasional overlay to the place where they had started.

Sydney considered the possibilities. One, that someone else had seen Edith Armstrong throw the note away and had gone to retrieve it, either out of curiosity or because he knew what it contained. Two, that an observant deputy had noticed it and picked it up on the time-honored principle that any object near a crime scene was potential evidence. Or three, a groundskeeper had removed it, as his job would require.

She studied the footprints a moment longer, then eliminated the third possibility. There weren't too many groundskeepers, surely, who performed their duties in smooth-soled dress shoes with pointed toes.

Neither was it likely that a deputy would wear shoes of that type. Of course, it might have been a plainclothesman or an evidence technician. Dwight Grant had been wearing dress shoes last night, but his foot size was proportionate to his height; these prints were too small.

If someone else had watched the note being thrown away, who was it?

Last night, during her interminable wait, she'd fixed the sequence of departures from Villa Saxon in her mind. The car following the Volvo had been Harrington's XJE, and behind it, Randall Day's Mercedes convertible.

She supposed that either man — or both — could have witnessed it.

It was equally possible that neither had, and some other agent was at work here.

Up the hill, the chauffeur had gotten out of the limousine. He removed his cap, smoothed his hair back, and replaced it, giving the brim a tug. Then he started toward her.

116

With one last glance at the footprints, Sydney headed up the hill. When she got to her office, she'd call Dwight Grant and tell him about the prints and the note. If he thought it was worth pursuing, he could send someone out to take photographs and plaster impressions.

Too bad she hadn't driven the Mustang, or she could get a set of photos for herself.

It was shortly before three-thirty when the limousine pulled into the parking lot. The lot was full of mothers running errands after picking the kids up from one of the three schools in the area, and after circling the lot once, the chauffeur gave up looking for a spot.

Leaving the engine idling, he got out and came around to open the door for her.

Luigi came to the door of his delicatessen, and stood behind the screen, wiping his hands on a blood-stained white towel and watching as the limo departed. "Moving up in the world, eh?" he said as she came closer.

"Not really." The smells wafting from the deli reminded her she hadn't eaten. "What's good today?"

"Everything," he said grandly. "Come and see for yourself."

Inside, the air was redolent with the aroma of fresh roast beef. She was ready to order a French dip to go when she remembered that this

117

was Wednesday. She was due at her mother's house tonight for dinner, and a roast topped the menu. What's more, dinner was only two hours off; she didn't dare fill up now.

"Egg salad, Luigi. On Squaw bread."

He clapped a big hand to his chest as though mortally wounded. "All of this, and you order *egg salad?* Life is too short for egg salad."

"Then why do you make it? Egg salad on Squaw bread and a Pepsi, please."

He muttered all the time he was preparing her sandwich. He wrapped the sandwich in wax paper and shoved it in a small paper bag with her drink. As he handed it to her, he said grudgingly, "It's very good egg salad."

Sydney gave him a five and waved off the change. "I'm looking forward to it."

The building supervisor, a graduate of the better-late-than-never school, had finally gotten around to putting up Christmas decorations, and she admired his handiwork as she went up the stairs. She couldn't really fault him for his tardiness, since she too was an alumni, traditionally doing her gift shopping on the twenty-fourth.

This year she'd made an exception, since her mother and Laura Ross were booked on a cruise to Acapulco, due to leave this Sunday.

Somehow or another, Mrs. Ross had persuaded Ethan to accompany them, and she expected her own mother to have one last go at convincing her. Neighbors since they'd both moved to San Diego as newlyweds following the second World War, Laura and her mother were as close as sisters.

Maybe closer.

It bothered them both that she and Ethan were estranged, and she suspected that they thought if they could get her and Ethan together for a romantic seven-day cruise that the sharp edges of their relationship could be worn down by the saltwater air.

Sydney shook her head, reaching the top of the stairs. What they didn't understand was that things had changed in the past few months. And it wasn't just Mitch's reappearance in her life that—

The door to her office was standing open.

She approached it cautiously, listening for any sounds that might indicate an intruder was still inside. But there was nothing.

Once at the doorway, she reached inside and turned on the seldom-used overhead fluorescents. They flickered briefly before flooding the room with light. The door to the darkroom was closed, as it had been when she left. The bathroom door was open, but she didn't remember it being otherwise.

On the surface, nothing seemed to have been disturbed. Her file cabinets were closed, the paperwork on her desk stacked neatly. There was none of the disorder that would suggest a search . . .

Sydney stepped inside.

At that instant, the phone rang. Her heart leapt into her throat, as if the ringing were the signal for all hell to break loose. In her mind's eye she pictured someone crashing through the darkroom door and rushing toward her, the way it happened in the movies.

Nothing of the kind occurred.

She took a deep breath and crossed to the desk, picking up the receiver on the third ring. "Bryant Investigations," she said, a little unsteadily.

"Sorry," that soft female voice whispered. "Wrong number."

If she hadn't paid two hundred dollars for the phone she would've thrown it through the window. Instead she slammed it down. She still had the brown paper bag in her hand, and she came close to throwing it instead. If she wasn't so thirsty, she would have.

"Son of a bitch," she swore, taking the Pepsi from the bag and popping the top.

Chapter Seventeen

Sydney went through the office, checking for signs of intrusion. The files were locked and didn't appear to have been forced, but to be sure, she opened the drawers one by one. There were hundreds of labelled case folders and it was impossible to tell at a glance if one—or ten—were missing, but she found no indication that the files had been rifled through.

She closed and locked the drawers.

There were half a dozen case files on her desk—the Saxon file among them—and she flipped through each. For once her obsession for organization paid off, because each file was arranged identically: face sheet, background information, interview notes, surveillance notes, and interim and final reports.

The categories were even color-coded, respectively white, yellow, green, blue, gray, and white again for the final report.

Besides the Saxon file, she'd pulled two files for review prior to scheduled court appearances after the first of the year, both divorce cases. The other three files were pending skip-traces, each of whom had apparently left the state.

Nothing appeared to be missing from any of the case folders. The binder of microfiche copies she'd collected on the Saxon family looked intact.

The desk drawers would offer little of interest for anyone prying; the two full-size drawers were where she kept blank forms, contracts, legal pads, and other supplies, and the top drawer contained sundry pens, pencils, hi-lighters, scissors, and the like.

Next she went to the shelves, running a finger across the spines of assorted reference books, Thomas Guides, and directories.

"What," she asked herself out loud, "you think some wild man broke in to look up a phone number because he couldn't get through to Directory Assistance?"

She went from the shelves to the darkroom, but that door was sturdily locked. The bathroom was empty, and unless her uninvited caller had a fetish for women's toiletries, she doubted it had drawn more than a glance.

That brought her back to the front door, which she'd left standing open. There were no marks on either lock, nor were there any on the striker plates. She touched the metal plates, considering what that meant.

Not that there was any doubt: it could only

mean that a professional had jimmied the locks.

Sydney stood, hands on her hips, and shook her head in confusion. Lack of sleep might have affected her thinking, but why would anyone break in and then not do what they'd come to do?

Maybe whoever it was had seen her arrive. The few minutes she'd spent in Luigi's Deli would have been adequate to cut and run.

She turned the knob on the deadbolt absently, listening to it slide solidly back and forth. Then she shut the door, and picked up the mail that had been pushed against the wall. Shuffling through envelopes as she returned to her desk, she heard the door open behind her.

"Deja vu," someone said.

Recognizing the voice, she turned. "Victor. I didn't expect to see you up and around for at least another twelve hours."

"I didn't expect to *be* up and around."

Under the circumstances, he didn't look any the worse for wear. He was dressed in the same clothes he'd worn last night, but his eyes were clear and his expression alert. His skin tone was on the pasty side, but then, that was normal for him.

I should be so lucky, she thought, feeling a delayed reaction as the adrenaline ebbed in her bloodstream, leaving her as limp as an old rag. She sat on a corner of the desk and tossed the envelopes into the 'in' basket. "How are you?"

"Fair to middling." He gave her a wan smile, walked in his ungainly style to the client chair and folded himself into it. His bony hands gripped his knees. "I wanted to thank you for caring enough to find me, and for staying with me while I went a little crazy—"

"Oh, Victor."

"Not everyone would have done that, you know. Compassion is . . . a rare commodity."

She had two reactions to that; first, that he was probably right, and second, that if he was right, it was a damned shame. "I wish I hadn't had to," she said. "I wish things had turned out differently."

"If wishes were horses . . ." His smile might have been engineered by an alien who had no comprehension of facial muscles and nerves. It was painful to look at, but she knew it hurt him more than it did her.

"So, Victor . . . what can I do for you?"

He flexed his fingers, tightened his grip on his knees. "I wondered if I might have the pictures you took of Martina. I know there'll be photos in the paper, but I'd rather not see those."

"Sure." Sydney shuffled again through the case folders on her desk and found the Saxon file. The photographs were tucked in a pocket inside the cover. She withdrew them and handed them across.

He accepted them reverently, as if they were the Holy Grail. "Thank you, Sydney. I don't have much to remember her by."

At a loss, she glanced down, scanning the top sheet of the case file. Had it been only two days ago when she'd filled it out?

"Actually, I don't have anything . . . but then, why should I?"

"Why shouldn't you?" she countered softly.

"Who am I kidding? Acting like a bereaved lover. Even if she wasn't . . . even if this hadn't happened, there wasn't a future for us."

Although she'd thought the same herself, she said, "You don't know that for sure."

"I know."

Sydney felt suddenly restless. She stood and began to pace, stopping momentarily to place her hand on his shoulder before moving past. "I wish I knew what to say."

"It doesn't matter."

"If it's any consolation, I think we'll find whoever killed her. The police—"

"We?"

"—haven't found anything to support the theory that it was a stranger who—"

"*We?*" Victor repeated incredulously. "As in, you and the police?"

"Turn that the other way around and you've got it. The sheriff's department gets top billing. The homicide team is obviously in charge, but I've been hired by Penelope Day Saxon."

"When did this happen?"

"Earlier today. As a matter of fact, I just got

back from there." She hadn't been looking at him while she paced, but now she did, and was surprised to see an angry frown on his face. "What's wrong?"

He acted as if he hadn't heard her question. "Why did you take the case, Sydney?"

"Why does any P.I. take any case?"

"I don't give a damn about any P.I.; I'm asking *you* why *you* took this case."

"I don't know . . . I guess I felt sorry for her, losing her granddaughter."

"Now you're feeling sorry for billionaires?" He laughed sarcastically. "What a joke."

"It isn't a joke." She noticed that he had crumpled the photographs of Martina in one big hand, and wondered whether it was a conscious act. "Anyway, don't you want to know what happened? Who killed her?"

"No, I absolutely do not want to know," he said, starting for the door.

She was between him and it, and she reached out for his arm, but he knocked her hand away and stormed past her. When she turned to look after him, she saw that he was shaking so violently he could hardly manage to open the door.

"Victor . . ."

"Leave me alone." He got the door open and stumbled across the threshold, then had to grab onto the wood balcony railing to keep from falling.

She followed him out of the office, but knew

she couldn't stop him.

He held onto the railing all the way to and down the stairs. His legs looked unsteady, as they had early this morning after he'd been drinking.

Afraid that he might fall, Sydney held her breath until he reached the bottom of the stairs. There he turned and gazed up at her with tortured eyes.

"Damn it, Sydney," he said, and wiped his eyes, his hand still clutching the photographs. "Damn it all to hell."

Then he was off again, lurching into the parking lot, weaving among the cars, oblivious to the shopping center traffic. He stepped in front of a beer truck, which missed him by inches, and the driver blasted the horn.

Sydney glanced away for a moment, trying to locate Victor's battered Dodge van in the lot, but not finding it. When she looked back, Victor had disappeared.

Chapter Eighteen

"Honey," Kathryn Bryant said, placing a cool hand against Sydney's flushed cheek, "if I had a cat, I'd expect to find it dragging you in."

"Thanks, Mom."

"Heavens, but you look exhausted."

Sydney took off her coat and hung it on a hook near the front door. "It's a ploy to get senior citizen's rates at the movies."

"Very clever, dear. Now go sit down, while I finish preparing dinner."

"Can I help?"

Her mother shook her head and gave her a gentle push in the direction of the sofa. "You cannot. Sit!"

"Mothers," Sydney said as she obeyed.

"Daughters." Her mother headed toward the kitchen, but stopped when she reached the door. "This'll take a few minutes; why don't you close your eyes and try to get a little rest?"

"I'm not tired," Sydney lied.

"If I had a nickel for every time you said that

as a child . . ." The words trailed off as, evidently confident that she'd gotten her point across, her mother slipped through the swinging door.

Sydney heard their voices in her mind, an echo from her childhood:

"Bedtime, Sydney."

"Can't I stay up just a little longer? Please, Mom? Please?"

"It's a school night, honey."

"But I'm not tired!"

"Maybe now you're not, but you will be in the morning if you don't get your rest."

"Mother!"

"Not another word, young lady. Off to bed with you now. 'Tis time to sleep."

Remembering, Sydney smiled and rested her head against the sofa cushions. There was no denying that it felt good to take a break . . . and it wouldn't hurt to close her eyes for a minute or two.

The melody of the door chimes brought her instantly awake. Like a fighter reacting instinctively to the sound of the bell, she was up and halfway there before it occurred to her who it must be at the door.

Her own mother had set her up.

Laura Ross stood beaming on the porch, her arms filled with brightly-wrapped packages, tied

129

with yards of curlicued ribbons. She had a sprig of mistletoe clipped in her hair, and a mischievous look in her eyes.

Ethan stood two steps behind his mother, holding a bottle of champagne bedecked with a huge green and red bow.

"Sydney," Laura Ross said, feigning surprise. "What an unexpected pleasure to find you here."

"Isn't it, though?" Sydney pushed the screen door open to let them in and accepted a kiss from her mother's dearest friend. "It's always nice to see you, Mrs. Ross . . . hello Ethan."

"Sydney." His gray eyes maintained their neutrality as he gave her a polite nod.

Lifting her chin, she held his gaze; she wouldn't be the one to look away.

"Who's that at the door?" her mother called. A moment later the kitchen door swung open and she came in, wiping her hands on her apron. "Oh, what a nice surprise. Laura and Ethan."

As if she hadn't orchestrated this down to the last detail. "Wear something nice," her mother had said. "That pretty red dress . . ."

Ethan looked away, and that allowed Sydney a chance to glare at her mother, whose eyes widened as she held up her hands in a pantomime of innocence.

Laura Ross laughed a trifle nervously and went to put the packages on the fireplace hearth. "I know we agreed not to decorate—and it *would* be a waste, since we won't be home for Christmas—but the room feels empty without a tree, doesn't it, Kathryn?"

"I suppose it does."

"And how about you, Sydney?" Mrs. Ross came and took both of Sydney's hands in hers. "I'm so sorry you won't be joining us on the cruise, but I hope you've made Christmas plans?"

"Actually, I—"

"Of course she has," Ethan interrupted. "How is Mitch, by the way?"

Her mother and Ethan's registered identical looks of alarm. If Ethan wasn't working so hard to annoy her, she might have laughed.

"Mitch is terrific," she said in her huskiest voice.

"Kathryn," Laura Ross said hurriedly, "we were just on our way to Ethan's office party and can't stay long, but we wanted to stop by for a holiday toast." She grabbed the champagne bottle from Ethan's hand with a shade more force than necessary.

"What a lovely idea," her mother said. "I'll get the good crystal—"

"Let me help you." Laura latched onto Kathryn's arm and nearly spun her around in her eagerness to be out of the room. They retreated into the kitchen, no doubt to devise a new strategy.

Sydney returned to the sofa and sat, ignoring

131

Ethan, who'd gone to stand by the fireplace with his back to her. She pulled at the skirt of her dress so that it would cover her knees, and then looked down at her bodice, all of a sudden aware of how much it revealed.

A fringe of black lace peeked from beneath the silky red material, both colors complimenting the creamy white of her skin.

It was too warm to put her coat back on, but she toyed with the thought that maybe she could find a sweater or a bathrobe or something to cover up with upstairs in her old bedroom. But that was ridiculous; why shouldn't she wear a sexy dress if she wanted to?

Then again, she *hadn't* wanted to. This dress was her mother's bright idea; after the day she'd had, she would have preferred well-worn, soft-as-butter jeans, a sweatshirt, and her Nikes. The hell with black pantyhose and four-inch heels.

Feeling rebellious, she kicked off the heels.

Ethan looked around at the sound.

Sydney flashed him a micro-smile. "I've had a long day," she said, even if it wasn't any of his concern. She rubbed a nyloned foot.

"Working," he said.

"What else?"

"I know Valentine tried to reach you a few times in the past few days."

"Really, a few times? She did leave one message on my machine, but I just haven't had the time lately to return calls."

"Haven't had time to return any calls or haven't had time to return my calls?"

Sydney kneaded a sore spot at the base of her middle toe and winced. "You haven't called."

"Calls from my office count as—"

"—calls from your office," she finished for him. "What did the inimitable Miss Lund want?"

Ethan sighed. "Your recipe for the rum punch you made for last year's Christmas party."

Although she felt she'd made her point, she was far from overjoyed about it. Last year seemed a very long time ago. "And the party's tonight. Do you want me to write it down for you?"

"I think she decided to go with that Hawaiian Punch stuff." He frowned while arching one eyebrow in that way that he had, as if to ask, Does the Environmental Protection Agency know about this shit?

The air in the room seemed almost to hum with tension, but this time Sydney did laugh. "There's always coffee."

It was a long-standing joke between them: Valentine Lund had many fine qualities, among them a ferocious sense of loyalty to her boss and an ironclad respect for the letter of the law—as every legal secretary should have—but her coffee could bring a two-hundred-and-fifty-pound stevedore trembling to his knees.

Ethan smiled.

Sydney glanced toward the kitchen door. The silence behind it was so absolute she would not have been surprised if both of their mothers fell through it, faces blue and half-asphyxiated from holding their breaths.

"I bought you a gift," she said, looking down at her hands. "It's out in the car. I was going to let Mom give it to you on the cruise."

"I'd rather you gave it to me." For the first time since they'd argued, she didn't hear anger in the tone of his voice.

Sydney got up. "I'll go get it, then." She nudged one of her high heels with her toe, but decided that they weren't worth the bother; she'd walk on the grass. She started for the front door.

"I could use a breath of air," Ethan said.

She merely nodded. At the door she switched on the porch light; the Mustang's interior lamp had burned out and she hadn't time to replace it.

They walked companionably enough across the lawn. The grass was slightly damp but it felt wonderful—cool and springy—beneath her feet.

All up and down the block, the houses were decorated for the season, and the multi-colored bulbs turned the fog into a confection of pastel light. The Morrisons displayed their familiar manger scene, which after twenty-five years looked a little worse for wear.

Sydney had been seven the year the manger had first appeared. Ethan, at fifteen, had been less enchanted than she was with the plaster figures, although at his mother's instruction, he'd taken Sydney's hand and walked her down the block to see it, after dark on Christmas Eve.

She remembered how it felt, looking up at him with complete trust that he would take care of her.

He was still trying to take care of her, she knew, and that was why he'd objected so vehemently to her relationship with Mitch, who'd hurt her badly once before. But Ethan could be stubborn and he refused to listen to her when she tried to tell him that she could take care of herself this time.

They'd arrived at the street and she was reaching for the door handle when she realized belatedly what it was that was different about her car. The driver's side window had been shattered, and the seat inside was covered with safety glass.

Ethan grabbed her by both shoulders and pulled her back. "Be careful, Sydney. You'll cut yourself."

"It's all right." Looking down, she didn't see any glass fragments on or around the concrete curb. She stood on the curb and opened the car door. A handful of glass rained down on the pavement.

Sydney reached behind the front seat for the

squeegee she kept there, and then used it to sweep what remained of her window into the street. She'd get a broom and dustpan from the house and clean it up later.

For now she retrieved the packages that were sitting in plain view on the back seat. She handed them to Ethan and closed the door.

"I don't understand," he said. "If someone wanted to steal these, why—"

"That's not what they wanted. The car wasn't locked, Ethan. It never is when I visit Mom."

"But if the door wasn't locked—"

"Why break the window?" She shook her head. "Someone's trying to get to me."

"Trying to scare you off? What cases are you working on?"

"There's no connection," she said, and glanced toward the house. "We'd better go in, or—"

"What makes you so sure there's no connection?"

"Because I'm only working one case, and this all started before I signed on." She took her packages back and headed for the porch.

Ethan came after her. "This *all?* You mean there's more?"

"It's nothing I can't handle."

"Sydney . . . talk to me."

"I'd rather not right now." She stepped gingerly on the porch—she'd gotten too many splinters from running barefoot up the stairs—

and saw through the screen door that her mother and Laura had returned to the living room with Mikasa flutes filled with champagne. She turned abruptly, and came face to face with Ethan.

Mere inches separated them, and she heard him take a sharp breath.

"Don't tell my mother about any of this," she whispered.

"I won't, but you're going to talk to me, do you hear? I want to know what's going on."

It was blackmail, plain and simple, and she knew she shouldn't stand for it. But with a gutter full of broken glass she had no choice. "Later," she said.

Chapter Nineteen

Later came sooner than she'd expected. When Sydney arrived at her apartment shortly before midnight, she found Ethan waiting at the wrought iron gate.

Coming from the shadows across the lawn, she saw him before he saw her, and she seriously considered ducking around the side of the building, climbing the seven foot fence — red dress, heels and all — and sneaking into the apartment by way of the laundry room, to which she had a key.

The last thing she needed right now was to be put through another inquisition.

Then he turned and saw her. "There you are. I was beginning to get worried."

"Ethan, it's late," she protested, "can't we talk some other time? Tomorrow or — "

"Now," he said firmly.

Sydney walked past him and unlocked the iron gate. Trouble, a neighbor's black and white long-haired tomcat, meowed at her from his position in the middle of the walk; knowing he was safe behind the narrow bars of the fence, the cat liked to taunt the occasional dog that happened by on the other side.

Ethan reached down and rubbed between the cat's ears. "Caught any mice lately?"

"He's not that kind of cat. Sara Lee, Pepperidge Farm, those are his favorites. He's particularly partial to the Champagne Collection."

"Can't say that I blame him." Ethan followed her down the hallway to her apartment.

"How was the party?" she asked absently, her mind on other things, in particular whether when she inserted her key in the deadbolt, she'd find the lock already open.

"Boring. I wonder why I put myself through it every year."

There were no outward signs of tampering, but already today she'd learned how little that meant. "Politics?"

"I suppose. Granted, every other lawyer in the building hosts a party, but what's the worst that could happen if I said enough is enough?"

The pins in the lock cylinder rotated smoothly as she gave the key a half-turn. "They wouldn't invite you to their parties?"

"You think so? The hell with it then."

She opened the door and stood with her back against it, allowing him to enter. "Do you want coffee?" She had a jar of instant she'd bought for guests.

Ethan ran a hand through his sandy hair. "It's

too late to be drinking coffee."

"Anything?" If memory served, she had on hand a can of Nestles hot chocolate, a box of cinnamon tea, skim milk, orange juice, and a case of Pepsi. She was ready to recite the list for him to select from when he took her hand and led her to the couch.

Facing her, he put a hand on each of her shoulders and looked at her for a long moment before giving her a gentle push. She sat down. He remained standing.

"Now, what's this all about?"

"I'm not exactly sure." She could see that he didn't care for her response. "The most obvious answer is that I've done something to annoy someone, and whoever it is has decided to harass me in return."

"You said there were other incidents?"

"A few."

When she didn't voluntarily elaborate, he prompted: "Such as what?"

"Phone calls, mostly." She outlined the dozens of supposed wrong numbers she'd received. Then, as if a dam had burst inside her, she heard herself spill the rest of it: the bloody vandalism, the warning call to her home number, and the break-in at her office. Figure in one broken window and the damage to her psyche was adding up.

"Nasty business," he said. "There's no logic to it, is there?"

"I haven't spent a lot of time looking for logic; this person is a nutcase."

"I don't know. Maybe not. There's a pattern there, a deliberate contradiction. Breaking the window of an unlocked car. Breaking and entering your office, but not disturbing anything."

"I think it's a felony to be analytical at this hour of the night."

He ignored her. "One warning to your home number and hundreds of supposedly innocuous wrong numbers at work. It's the reverse of what you might expect. The blood balloon was something of an anomaly, though."

"Whatever." Sydney covered her mouth to hide a yawn. Exhaustion caused her eyes to tear and she wiped at them. "Anyway, so now you know everything that I know. Would it be too much to ask to let me get some sleep?"

"There are probably just the two of them, a man and a woman. There could be others, but I doubt it; this kind of thing requires a common purpose, and—"

"Ethan, we're not going to solve this tonight. I've been awake for—" it took her brain a sluggish moment to calculate "—about forty-one hours."

"This is serious," he said. "There's no guarantee that they won't try to hurt you."

"I can take care of myself."

"That remains to be seen. How much of this have you reported to the police?"

Exasperated by his persistence, Sydney slapped a hand to her forehead and slumped sideways on the couch, which in a pinch could substitute for her bed. She moved her hand to cover her eyes. Maybe he'd go away.

The cushion sank a few inches as Ethan sat beside her. "You have reported it, haven't you?"

She spread her fingers and peeked through at him. "Not to the police. I think I mailed the wrong number log to the phone company. Or if I didn't, I meant to."

"That's comforting."

"Listen, I know people like this—"

"And I don't? I was a cop for seven years."

"—and they do mean little things because they have mean little minds, but eventually they'll run out of ideas or get tired of the game."

"It's not a game, Sydney."

"I think it is. And I think whoever is behind it is basically a coward."

"Give a coward a gun . . ." Ethan said and then let the rest go unspoken.

She'd heard the phrase so often that her traitorous brain finished it: *Give a coward a gun and what did you have? A sniper.*

"This is just what I needed to hear right now." She propped herself up and brushed the hair out of her face. "What ever happened to 'Sweet dreams'?"

"That's Mitch's department now."

Four words, and Ethan's face was transformed

into that of a stranger. The years of shared history disappeared under the accusation in his eyes.

Sydney got up quickly from the couch. When she was nearly to her bedroom door, she turned. She didn't want to talk about this, but she couldn't stop herself. "Damn you, Ethan, for once and for all, I am not sleeping with Mitch Travis."

"You say that, but—"

"But nothing. We're dating, all right? We go out to dinner, to a show, maybe for a walk on the beach. Then he brings me home, and we say goodnight at the door. That's it."

Ethan stood but remained where he was. "I shared a squad car with Mitch for most of my years on the force. I know him . . . and he isn't the type to be satisfied with a chaste kiss at the door."

"Forever? No, he probably isn't. But for now, that's all there is between us."

"Even if that's true—"

"It *is* true."

"—he's no good for you."

She glared at him. "Would you like to check the birthdate on my driver's license? You seem to be under the mistaken impression that I'm still a child."

"I didn't say that."

"Or maybe you think I'm feeble-minded, and I can't be trusted to make my own decisions?"

"What I think is, you've allowed your physical attraction to Mitch to overwhelm your common sense." Ethan cleared his throat. "And I also think you're using Mitch to get back at me."

"At you?"

"I don't think you've ever forgiven me for marrying Jennifer while you were working in Los Angeles."

Jennifer was his ex-wife, whom he'd met, married, and divorced, all within a year. Since she'd never met the woman, never even seen a photograph of her—Ethan had burned the wedding pictures—it seemed absurd to be accused of being jealous of her . . .

Nevertheless, Sydney assimilated that charge with the others, and for the first time in her life she wished that Ethan would just go away.

Is he too close to the truth? a voice in her mind asked.

"I think you'd better leave," she said as calmly as she could manage.

Chapter Twenty

Thursday

After a restless night of sleep interrupted by moments of sudden wakefulness, Sydney began the morning by dropping the Mustang off at the Lincoln-Mercury dealership on Miramar Road for repairs. She transferred a few essentials—her tool kit and the Smith and Wesson—from the Mustang to the black Thunderbird she'd rented.

She went next to the sheriff's substation, intending to make a brief amendment to her statement to include the piece of paper Edith Armstrong had thrown away on the night of the murder. And she'd at least mention the footprints by the side of the road.

It was unfortunate that she'd forgotten to report them yesterday, because there was a chance that since then they might have disappeared—a brisk wind would have erased them — but those were the breaks.

She planned to be in and out of the substation in fifteen minutes.

Dwight Grant cut her off at the pass.

"Miss Bryant," he said, his voice loud enough to rattle the windows. "Just the person I wanted to see. I'd like a word with you."

The deputy manning the front office gave her a sympathetic look and then reached to answer the phone which had been ringing when she'd walked in.

She followed Grant obediently though the narrow hall to his office. Daylight hadn't improved the aesthetics of the place, which was painted an awful institutional duo of green and beige.

Grant closed the door behind them and gestured to the chair opposite his desk. His own chair screeched in protest as he lowered his bulk into it. He leaned forward and opened a cobalt blue, hard-cover file, the kind with three dividers and metal clasps inside. He flipped through the pages, pausing occasionally to read.

Sydney took advantage of the opportunity to glance around the office. There were framed photographs on the wall of the current and past sheriffs, as well as several showing Grant with

146

various local big-wigs. There was a diploma from the Academy, and a B.A. in Criminal Justice from the California State University at Fullerton.

There was also a commendation for bravery above and beyond the call of duty. An 'attaboy' in the police vernacular.

There were six four-drawer filing cabinets along one wall, and stacked on top were hundreds of folders in several piles which were listing precariously to one side. On top of the shortest pile was a half-eaten jelly donut on a crumpled blue paper napkin.

The desk itself held an assortment of so-called executive games, among them a tri-level acrylic chess set with polished granite pieces, one of those perpetual motion toys with the six silver balls, and a Chinese puzzle box. An ornate beer stein was crammed with pens and, oddly enough, a bunch of Snoopy pencils.

"I heard from Mrs. Saxon yesterday," Grant said, reclaiming her attention. "She told me that she'd hired you, and why. I listened to her reasons and then did my best to talk her out of it."

Sydney inclined her head to acknowledge that she had anticipated his reaction.

"But Mrs. Saxon is a four-hundred-pound gorilla in this city; she does whatever she wants to, and nobody tells her 'no'."

"I couldn't," she agreed.

"Now, I'm going to be honest with you; I don't think you — or any private investigator — has any business being involved in a murder case."

"That doesn't exactly come as a shock to me," she said evenly.

"I didn't think it would." He rapped the open file with his knuckles. "Having said that, I should add that I don't want you underfoot while I'm working the case."

"I won't be," she said, and smiled. What did he think, that she was going to play pilot fish to his shark, picking information like shreds of flesh from between his razor-sharp teeth?

"Because the sheriff has emphatically suggested that I do so, I have agreed, however reluctantly, to let you review the case file from time to time. I'm not happy about it, and if any material of a confidential nature finds its way to the press, for instance, I will do my damnedest to get your license pulled."

"Understood."

"Good." He closed the file and started to hand it to her, then pulled back. "One last thing, and I'll send you on your way."

Sydney suppressed a sigh.

"In the unlikely event that you should discover, to a high degree of certainty, the identity of Martina Saxon's killer, you are to take *no* action on your own. Repeat, *no* action. Call us!"

"Of course. That is, assuming that circumstances don't force my hand."

It evidently wasn't what he wanted to hear and he showed his displeasure by scowling fiercely at her. "What circumstances do you have in mind?"

"If I'm backed into a corner, I'll have to do whatever it takes to get out of harm's way." It would be, she thought, a simple matter of self defense.

If anything, Grant's expression darkened. "Is that right? Well, I'm going to go way out on a limb here, and suggest that you stay out of rooms with corners."

"I'll do my best."

Dwight Grant regarded her for the better part of a minute before finally handing the folder across. "If I were you, Miss Bryant, I'd fade away into the background and let us do *our* jobs. Pull one of those 'Let's don't, and say we did' scams."

"Mrs. Saxon expects me to report to her directly. She strikes me as a woman who expects to get fair value for her money." Sydney got up, the file in hand. "Now . . . is there some place I can read this in privacy?"

Grant shrugged. "Find an empty interrogation room."

She turned to go.

"And don't forget to return the file to my office when you're finished."

Chapter Twenty-one

The interrogation room was not designed for the mental, emotional, or physical comfort of those brought in for questioning. The amenities consisted of a wood table and four metal chairs with cracked vinyl cushions. A plastic ashtray on the table was full to overflowing with cigarette butts, and there were several styrofoam cups with varying amounts of stale coffee in them.

The air in the room was musty, redolent with a miasma of cigarette smoke, human perspiration, and dread. There were no windows and a single small air vent supplied what ventilation there was.

Sydney poured the coffee dregs into one cup and then nested the others beneath. There wasn't a waste basket, so she put them aside, and shoved the ashtray to the farthest corner of the table. A fine ring of ash marked where it had been.

She sat down then and opened the case file.

The first deputy on the scene had submitted a brief report, detailing his actions from the moment he'd received the call. She was amused to find herself misidentified as "Sidney Brant, female P.E."

Spelling skills had never been and still weren't a top priority in police recruiting. Ditto for typing: there were entire lines x'd out.

The narrative was written in the awkward, sketchy style peculiar to police reports. There wasn't much in it that she didn't already know, but she read it carefully for the sake of thoroughness.

The reports filed by other deputies responding to the call were similar in content and form, revealing little more than their strict adherence to standard police procedures. If Dwight Grant had written a preliminary report—which she strongly suspected he had—it hadn't been included in the file.

"How did that happen?" she wondered aloud, and imagined Grant's laconic reply: "An oversight."

She flipped to the middle section of the folder. The autopsy report was five pages long including the face sheet, which listed the death as a homicide and gave the cause as multiple stab wounds.

Sydney turned the page. It wasn't often that she had access to this type of information, and she felt a sick fascination as she began to read:

General

This is a well-developed, well-nourished Caucasian female who appears to be her stated age of twenty-two. Weight is approximately 115 pounds, and height is measured at 66 inches.

Clothing

The body is received in a white full slip of a nylon material. Both straps are intact, and the seams of the garment have not been torn. There are seven cuts in the fabric, consistent with the incised wounds visualized on the right and left upper torso. The smallest is 3.5 centimeters in length, the largest is 4.5 centimeters. Bloodstains are present. On the right fourth finger is a yellow metal and purple stone ring.

External Examination

The hair is straight, blond, and of shoulder-length. It is damp when the body is presented, and smells faintly of chlorine. The irides are brown; the pupils are fixed, regular and equal in dilation. A white foamy substance is exuding from both nostrils. There is a small amount of clotted blood in the mouth. All teeth are present and in a good state of repair. Examination of the external auditory canals is unremarkable; however the right tympanic membrane is mildly inflamed and bulging slightly. The chest is symmetrical, breasts are small and symmetrical, and the abdomen is flat. The extremities are normal. An examination of the upper- and mid-back regions of the body reveals multiple stab wounds.

There was a great deal more—the stab wounds were described individually in nauseating detail—but Sydney found it difficult to read the cold clinical recital of mortal wounds. She skimmed through the lengthy internal examination section also, with its references to aortal lacerations and hemorrhages, the presence of massive quantities of blood—and a lesser amount of chlorinated water—in the lungs and pleural cavity, and evidence of cardiac and respiratory failure secondary to exsanguination.

Interpreted, it meant that Martina had bled to death before she could drown.

With her head propped up in both hands, Sydney reviewed the autopsy surgeon's meticulous inspection of the internal organs, which, as expected in a healthy young woman, showed no signs of disease or defect. Specimens were taken and preserved in formaldehyde for the pathologist to examine, and blood and urine samples were collected for toxicologic analysis. Stomach contents were preserved.

Although there'd been no indication of sexual violation, smears were taken from the mouth, vagina, and rectum. Two paragraphs down, the

154

microscopic exams were reported to be negative.

The toxicology results were pending, but they'd requested tests of Martina's bodily fluids for the presence of alcohol, barbiturates, stimulants, tranquilizers, and — strangely, Sydney thought — narcotics.

Another curiosity: not even an estimation of the time of death was given.

When Sydney finished the postmortem report, she closed her eyes. It would be so damned easy to let the brutal details desensitize her, thus transforming Martina from a person into a specimen. It certainly was easier not to envision a face when reading of the human body's systematic dissection.

A few minutes passed before she went on.

The third and final section of the folder contained witness statements. She was somewhat surprised to find that there were only three of them, and that her own statement was one of the three. The other two were those given by Jared Saxon and his mother, Miss Penelope.

Where was Owen Saxon's statement? She knew it existed, because she'd seen it — in Dwight Grant's possession — on the night of Martina's death.

That aside, why hadn't the police conducted more interviews by now? The murder was over thirty-six hours old, and there'd been plenty of time to talk to virtually everyone in the Saxon household.

Perhaps the homicide investigators were holding off in deference to the family's grief. It certainly was possible that Miss Penelope's friends in high places had interceded here as well. Or maybe the interviews *had* been done, but hadn't yet been transcribed.

Or Dwight Grant had yanked them from the file for reasons known only to himself.

Sydney had a hunch that of those possibilities, the last was the most likely.

She closed the file and drummed her fingers on the table, contemplating her next move. Should she accuse Grant of withholding information, and then duck while he hit the roof? If she was wrong, she risked endangering a very shaky alliance.

For that matter, she'd likely be risking the same response even if she was right.

Besides, she reasoned, it wasn't as though she'd intended to rely heavily on the police interviews; she had every intention of conducting her own investigation from start to finish. At best, reviewing the statements might have given her a heads-up as to the veracity of those she spoke with.

There were other ways to determine truthfulness. Many other ways.

Chapter Twenty-two

David Saxon had found a unique way to deal with the stress of his sister's death: facing a seemingly endless volley of tennis balls on one of the Villa's immaculate grass courts.

Sydney stood, her fingers entwined in the chain-link fence, watching as he braved the onslaught, responding with speed and grace to every pitched ball. Despite its rapid-fire pace and high velocity, the automatic server was no match for him.

The man had a wicked backhand.

In minutes, the opposite side of the court was a sea of bright yellow tennis balls.

Eventually, though, the machine ran out of ammunition. David wiped his forehead with the sweatband on his wrist and then started toward the net, presumably to re-load and have another go at it.

"Excuse me," Sydney called, "may I talk to you for a few minutes?"

Evidently he hadn't been aware that anyone

was watching; he visibly started at the sound of her voice. She felt a kind of perverse satisfaction in his reaction, no doubt because people had been sneaking up on and surprising her for days now.

After a brief hesitation, he nodded, then walked in her direction. "You're the detective," he said when he reached the fence.

"Yes. Sydney Bryant." She extended her hand and then realized that he intended to keep the gate — which was locked — between them. So she drew back and stuck both of her hands in her jacket pockets.

"Grandmother said you'd want to talk to me." His sports bag was on the ground near the gate and he reached down for a fluffy white towel. "But I'm not sure that I'll be of any assistance."

"You never can tell," she said, more philosophically than she felt, and decided to get right to it: "When I spoke with Owen, he mentioned that you and he had an argument at dinner that night."

"Another argument, yes." He pressed the towel over his face and held it there for thirty or forty seconds. When he lowered it, the flush of exertion had faded and his skin was dry.

What well-mannered sweat glands, Sydney thought.

"The problem with Owen," David Saxon said, "is that he was born with a sense of entitle-

158

ment. He thinks he should have whatever he wants, when he wants it. He thinks it's his due."

Sydney smiled. "And yourself?"

"I don't mind working for what I get."

"What about Martina?"

A pained look crossed his face. He wadded the towel into a ball and dropped it onto the grass near the bag. "My sister didn't care much for being rich. People treated her differently, she said, when they knew she came from money. She hated that."

"Is that why she worked at the newspaper?"

"I don't know. I suppose it could have been *a* reason, if not *the* reason. But that isn't what you wanted to talk to me about, is it?"

Sydney recognized the impatience in his voice, and moved along. "On the night your sister was killed . . . Owen said that Martina was still at the table when he left. Is that how you remember it?"

David Saxon shrugged. "I suppose. I know he stormed out of the dining room before dessert was served. I only remember that because the cook had prepared a raspberry bombe at Owen's request, and she was disappointed that he wasn't there to enjoy it. Not that that's unusual. My brother has a real knack for disappointing people. A gift, you might say."

"Did Martina have dessert?" The analysis of stomach contents would confirm that.

He took his time answering, staring off in the distance and blinking every few seconds. "No," he said finally, his tone positive. "She wasn't there. She must have left right after Owen."

That was interesting. Did that mean she'd gone after him, or was it merely a coincidence? "Did you see her after dinner?"

"I'm afraid not."

"What did you do, then?"

"Why, I . . . I went to dress."

"Did you see anyone else?"

For the first time, David Saxon looked a little uneasy. "Not that I recall. No, wait a minute. Felice, I talked to Felice."

"Where was this?"

"Her room, or rather one of the guest rooms. She's staying with us for the holidays."

"You talked in her room?"

"Actually, we talked through the door. I wanted to make sure she hadn't changed her mind again about what she was going to wear."

Sydney shook her head. "Why would it matter what she wore?"

"Mother was loaning her a sapphire necklace and earrings. As beautiful as the gems are, it wouldn't do for them to clash with her gown."

Sydney could hear Victor's voice taunt: *Who says the rich don't have problems like the rest of us?*

"Anyway, she was just ready to take her

shower, and wouldn't open the door."

She regarded him with a hint of skepticism. "Is she that shy?"

David Saxon clearly understood what she was really asking, and he thrust out his square jaw. "When appropriate, yes, she is. This is my grandmother's house, Miss Bryant, and we respect her wishes."

Fair enough, Sydney thought. "What time did you talk to your fiance?"

"I don't know." He smiled wryly. "I didn't think to look at my watch."

Overhead, a cloud passed in front of the sun and the air cooled noticeably. Sydney zipped up her jacket and turned up the collar. Dressed as he was in tennis shorts and a thin cotton shirt, she wondered why he wasn't shivering. Maybe blue blood ran warmer than red . . .

"Is that all?" he asked.

"Not quite. Do you have any idea about who might have killed Martina?"

He flinched, his mouth drawing tight with distaste. "I do not."

"I'm sure by now you realize that it had to have been someone at the house that night."

"I'm not a fool, Miss Bryant. As much as it saddens me, I have thought about it. We all have."

"But you haven't reached a conclusion?"

"Only that two lives will have been ruined by my sister's death."

She hadn't expected him to be that insightful. "There's no one she'd been arguing with?"

"At one time or another, I'd dare say we've all argued with each other . . . but recently? No. As a matter of fact, I would suggest that of late we've been getting along very well. Except for Owen and myself, and I don't see how our troubles could possibly have anything to do with her . . . with the . . ."

Seeing that he was having difficulty with the word, she said it for him: "Murder."

"There were ten of us here that night," he said quickly, as if he wanted to change the subject. "Thirteen if you count the help—"

"Which of the help?"

"Edith, of course, and Virgil, he's Grandmother's chauffeur. And the cook, Margaret."

Sydney frowned. The chauffeur had been driving the limousine, and she'd seen Edith leave, but where had the cook disappeared to? "Does Margaret drive a Jeep?"

"A Jeep? Margaret?" He appeared momentarily confused and then his expression cleared. "Oh no, that's Chad's car."

Another name she wasn't familiar with. "And who is Chad?"

"Our cousin. Chad Fuller. His mother is our mother's sister."

All of these relatives! It would take some doing to keep them straight. "Is Chad staying at Villa Saxon as well?"

"Not at all. His family lives in Fallbrook, but my aunt and uncle are vacationing in Great Britain, and he's been at loose ends lately." A tiny crease appeared on David Saxon's forehead. "He tends to get in trouble when left to his own devices. I think Owen invited him to a private party after the Festival."

"I see. If I might backtrack for a moment . . . Margaret wasn't in the house when I . . . when the police arrived, but I didn't see her leave."

"Margaret left with my grandmother. Her quarters are on the southern-most edge of the property."

That was unexpected; Sydney hadn't considered the possibility that there were accommodations for the help on the grounds.

"Margaret usually walks home—she says it keeps her young—but dinner was late and Grandmother insisted on giving her a ride. Margaret's been with us since well before I was born," he said somewhat primly, as if to counter the notion that the servants were accustomed to limousine rides and other favors.

Sydney mentally added the cook's name to her list of people to talk to. And Chad Fuller, she reminded herself. "About Martina," she be-

163

gan, and then noticed that she no longer had David Saxon's undivided, albeit reluctant, attention.

He had reached into the sports bag and brought out a key, and was now in the process of unlocking the tennis court gate. "Felice," he said, and smiled. The smile transformed his face from just this side of plain to almost, but not quite, handsome.

Sydney turned to see Felice McDaniel coming their way. Like a chameleon, she had changed her coloration again; today, she wore her short dark hair in tight curls, and the dramatic red lipstick of the night before last had been replaced by a very feminine pale pink.

Her eyes were a feline green.

She was dressed in an off-white jumpsuit that accentuated her slim build, and had a navy blue sweater draped over her shoulders. "David, here you are," she said in a voice that managed to be husky and whispery at the same time.

"I was just coming up to the house." He glanced at Sydney as though surprised to find her still there. "Miss Bryant, this is my fiance, Felice McDaniel. Felice, Miss Bryant is—"

"A private investigator." Felice offered her hand and looked intently into Sydney's eyes. "What a fascinating line of work."

"It often is."

"I can imagine." Felice hooked her arm

through David's and caught him in her gaze. "But you'll have to excuse us for now, or we'll be late for our counseling session, right darling?"

"That's right."

Watching them as they walked away arm-in-arm, she had more than an inkling as to who had the advantage in their relationship; for all of his wealth and position, if he had a tail, David Saxon would have wagged it at the sound of his mistress's voice, or at the very least been nipping at her heels.

For his sake, she hoped he did nothing to displease his fiance, who looked to Sydney like she was entirely capable of kicking her darling in the teeth.

Chapter Twenty-three

Amanda Saxon had taken to her bed after her daughter's death, and only through the intervention of Miss Penelope had she agreed to a brief interview.

Sydney followed Edith Armstrong through the silent hallway to a private suite of rooms in the northwest corner of the mansion. The housekeeper had not yet spoken a word, and Sydney wondered whether she'd been reprimanded after Boyd Harrington had come upon them in the kitchen.

Or possibly she felt she'd said too much without giving thought to the consequences . . .

Whatever the reason, Sydney would have to find a way to finish their earlier conversation. The housekeeper's cryptic remarks about Harrington intrigued her.

They had reached a set of double doors, painted white with gold trim in a French Provincial style that seemed at odds with the hacienda motif. The ornate crystal door knobs acted as prisms, casting a rainbow spectrum of colors on the polished wood floor.

Sydney glanced up to find the light source; three spotlights were recessed into the ceiling, bathing the doors in a warm glow.

Edith knocked twice on the door, then folded her hands quietly in front of her.

A few moments later, the door opened, and a woman in a nurse's uniform exchanged a nod with the housekeeper, then stepped aside to let them in.

The suite's parlor was one of the least inviting rooms Sydney had ever seen. With its incredibly ugly period furnishings and heavy velvet drapery, it was the kind of room that usually could be found roped off at museums, although to her it was a toss-up as to whether those rooms were being protected from the museum-goers or vice versa.

There were flowers everywhere, and the air was thick with a heady blend of fragrances. The astringent scent of roses seemed predominant.

"Is she awake?" Edith asked the nurse.

The nurse, a solid, stocky woman with a broad Slavic face, nodded. "Yes, and there's the pity. I don't think she's slept more than an hour or so at a time these past two nights."

"The doctor was here?"

Again the nurse nodded. "He's given her a sedative, but the poor dear's fighting it. Doesn't

167

want to sleep, she says. Nightmares, I'm guessing."

"I shouldn't wonder." Edith turned to Sydney. "I hope you can do this quickly and . . . gently."

"Perhaps I should come back another time," she offered. She wasn't all that eager to intrude on a mother's grief. "A better time."

"There may not be a better time for a long while," the nurse said. "And to be honest, I think it may do her some good to talk about it. Holding her feelings in the way she has been isn't healthy. A good cry might do her a world of good."

Sydney could understand that, but the prospect of being present when Amanda Saxon broke into tears wasn't one she welcomed. Still, she was here now, and Mrs. Saxon *had* agreed to see her.

"I won't be long," she said.

Amanda Saxon was not in her canopied bed, but rather was standing near a window which looked out on a small private patio. Dressed in a peach gown with matching robe, she was so pale that even the reflected pink-gold glow from the silk did not warm her complexion.

Martina had inherited her mother's striking good looks down to but one detail: Amanda's

168

eyes were a deep clear blue instead of brown.

Owen had his mother's eyes, Sydney noted. Except his hadn't been filled with pain.

"Mrs. Saxon, thank you for seeing me."

"I hadn't a choice," Amanda Saxon said evenly. "But that isn't your fault."

Momentarily unnerved, Sydney didn't reply.

"My husband's mother has never shied from imposing her will on others . . . I expect that she has already decided how many days I'll be allowed to mourn for Martina, and when they've passed, she'll send an emissary to return me to the fold."

There was a lack of bitterness in the woman's voice, which Sydney found curious, if what she said was true. "I understand that it must be difficult for you to talk about your daughter's death, but I ·have a few questions if you're up to—"

"Excuse me," Amanda Saxon said, touching her fingertips to her face which had gone a bloodless white, "but I must sit down."

Sydney grabbed her before she could fall, and helped her to a nearby chair. "Should I call the nurse?"

"No, I'll be fine, I just . . . felt faint."

Taking Amanda's hand in both of hers, Sydney was alarmed by the coldness of her skin. "The nurse said you'd had a sedative; would you rather lie down?"

169

"Not yet. Not yet." She closed her eyes and seemed visibly to gather her composure. A minute later, she looked at Sydney and actually smiled.

Amazed at her resiliency, Sydney smiled back.

"Go ahead, and ask your questions, Miss . . . I'm so sorry, but I'm afraid I've forgotten your name."

"Sydney Bryant."

"Sit down, Miss Bryant—"

"I prefer Sydney."

"Sydney then." A hint of color had appeared on her cheekbones. "I'll do anything I can to help find whoever did this . . . sit down and ask your questions."

Sydney pulled a chair near. "If you're sure it won't upset you . . ."

"Finding my daughter's killer is worth it at any price."

"All right then. I've been told that on Tuesday night at dinner, David and Owen were having a disagreement."

"On Tuesday night," Amanda Saxon nodded, "and on Monday, Sunday, and Saturday nights before that. In any seven day period, I'd guess that on six of them, my sons would be at each other's throat."

"I see. I've also been told that Martina left the table shortly after Owen did. Is that how you remember it?"

"I believe so, yes."

"Can you tell me . . . was she going after her brother, do you think?"

"I'm not sure I can answer that," she said, and paused. "Martina often played the peacemaker between David and Owen—and as you can imagine, there was quite frequently peace to be made—but looking back, I'd have to say that on *that* evening, she probably wasn't even aware that they were arguing."

"Really?"

"Absolutely. She seemed very distracted that evening. Of all my children, Martina is . . . was the most opinionated. She was remarkably adept at making her feelings known, and under normal circumstances, she would have entered the fray between her brothers. She said nothing."

"Do you know—"

"What was bothering her? Or who? I wish I did. Whatever it was, it ruined her appetite. She barely touched her dinner."

"Did she act like she was angry?"

"Not angry," she said, a quizzical look on her face. "More . . . disappointed. Even defeated somehow. I thought at the time that she looked sad . . ."

Sydney wasn't sure how to fit that into a confrontation that would ultimately end in Martina's death. Motive might not be a requirement of law in convicting a person of murder, but there had to be a reason that someone plunged a knife repeatedly into her back.

The crime was too savage to have been committed in cold blood.

With that in mind, she asked, "Had she had any disagreements with anyone that you know of in the past few weeks?"

"Not that recent. Lately she's been all caught up in her work."

"At the newspaper," Sydney mused.

"She loved that job. Ever since she was a little girl, she wanted to be a journalist."

"And she could be anything she wanted."

Amanda inclined her head. "None of the children lacked opportunity. David took the safe path in a family business. Owen preferred not to take any path at all. But Martina . . . she blazed her own trail."

The pride in Amanda Saxon's eyes shone behind unshed tears, and Sydney felt her throat constrict in sympathy. She wanted very much to have this over with, but she had a nagging sense that if she listened, she might pick up a thread to begin unraveling this case.

So she persisted. "You said a minute ago that Martina hadn't argued with anyone recently. What about before that? Say, in the last six months."

"Oh, my. Well. The first person who comes to

172

mind is Uncle Randall. Last July they had a falling out . . ."

"About what?"

"Have you met Randall Day yet?"

"No." Sydney visualized him as he'd been the night Martina was murdered, driving in a convertible with the top down, and singing a country western song with all of his might. He didn't fit her picture of a killer.

"Randall is the eccentric in the family. He does everything to excess. Plays the horses, but badly. Drinks more than he should. He's extravagant with money, throws it around without a second thought. His *friends*—male or female—are little more than leeches. I shouldn't be saying these things, but the man will drive you crazy."

"He drove Martina crazy?"

"Martina adored him. He has a certain charm about him, I can't deny that, but charm has its limits."

Harrington would fault her for asking leading questions, but she couldn't resist: "And Martina reached the limit last summer?"

"Yes. It seems he'd been borrowing money from her—"

"I thought he was wealthy in his own right."

"He has a trust fund, but the way he spends money, he's frequently short of cash. Martina was a soft touch for him; he'd give her some

173

story or another and she'd loan him a few hundred here and there."

"What happened?"

Amanda sighed. "I don't know the whole story. Martina had been after him for some time to give up drinking, and he swore that he would. Then on the Fourth of July, he was arrested for drunk driving . . ."

"I remember reading about that," Sydney said.

"She went down and bailed him out, and I guess on the way home, they had it out. They didn't speak to each other for the longest time."

"Did they make up?"

"More or less. But I don't think she's loaned him a dime since."

Money, Sydney thought. She wondered if by chance Martina had a will, and if so, whether Uncle Randall was named. "Besides Randall Day, is there anyone else that she argued with?"

"Nothing as dramatic. She needled Owen once in a while about getting a job. She did have a word or two with Chad, but Chad is forever testing one's patience."

"How is that?"

"I think you'll see for yourself when you meet him—" Amanda took a sudden deep breath and brought her hand to her chest.

"Are you all right?"

"I'm just a little dizzy. The medication must be taking effect."

Sydney felt guilty for keeping her talking so long. "Let me call the nurse for you."

This time there was no argument. Amanda leaned back in the chair and closed her eyes.

Chapter Twenty-four

While Edith and the nurse were busy helping Amanda Saxon into bed, Sydney took the opportunity to embark on an unescorted tour of Villa Saxon. In particular, she was interested in the rooms that opened into the courtyard where Martina had been slain.

It struck her as odd that a homicide had been committed at the architectural center of the house—a center surrounded by glass—and no one had seen what happened.

Or heard. Even double-paned windows were poor filters of sound, and unless the murderous act had been played out in absolute silence—and that thought chilled her blood—someone should have heard.

Sydney walked quickly down the hallway. On the way in, she'd noticed a residue of some sort on one of the doors; she suspected that it was adhesive from the official paper seal the police used on the door. The seal itself had been removed, and no doubt so had every possible thing which might prove to be evidence.

Regardless, she wanted a look.

At the door, she ran her fingertips over the wood for confirmation, and felt a slight stickiness. She turned the knob and then ducked inside, closing the door silently behind her.

Immediately she thought of the photographs she'd taken of Martina; the room was decorated in shades of gray. The carpet was a dark charcoal, the bedspread and curtains were a lighter ash, and the wallpaper was luminescent pearl gray. The only splash of color in the room was a purple shawl which had been tossed on the bed.

The room was furnished sparely with only a bed, night table, a couple of wall-mounted shelves, and a rattan swing which was suspended from the ceiling near the sliding glass door. There was a walk-in closet with custom cedar drawers built in, and next to it a bathroom with a sunken tub, separate shower, a coral-pink sink shaped like a seashell, and the vanity. On the vanity, a dozen or more perfume bottles were displayed on a mirrored tray.

The scent of Fever persisted in the air.

There wasn't much in the way of personal belongings visible: a paperback copy of Capote's *In Cold Blood* on the night table; a stuffed toy shark on the pillow; a goldfish bowl that was full of matchbooks and boxes; and an old-fashioned gum ball machine.

Sydney went to draw the curtain back from the sliding glass door. Clouds had been drifting inland all morning and only thin rays of sunlight shone through.

In the courtyard, the pool reflected the darkening sky. Without the underwater lights on, the pool appeared murky and bottomless.

She slipped back the latch on the door and pulled it open. There was a screen, but it hadn't been closed fully, and she stepped through the narrow opening.

Misting machines sprayed aerated water on the lush green plants. The mist collected into glistening beads on leaves and fronds, eventually dripping onto the tiles.

What had brought Martina out here? Barefoot, dressed only in a slip, why had she left her room? Hadn't she known how vulnerable she was? Hadn't she felt the stirrings of fear?

Or was it that she simply had never thought it could happen to her?

Sydney stood in silence. Listening, but unsure of for what. Echoes of violence, a stifled scream, the wet sound of a knife blade, slick with blood . . .

She shivered but resisted the impulse to go inside.

What had brought Martina out here?

Sydney was no closer to an answer when she returned to Martina's room.

Force of habit drove her to search the room,

uncertain of what she was searching for, but hopeful that she'd know it when—and if—she saw it.

The police had presumably removed any diaries or journals, as well as recent correspondence. She found an address book in the night stand drawer, but since the killer had to be one of the thirteen in the house at the time of the murder, it was unlikely that the address book would be of value.

She went next to the closet, in which a boutique's worth of blouses, sweaters, skirts, pants, and dresses were hung in separate sections. She lacked the ability to identify a specific designer's line at a glance, but she could tell that Martina hadn't shopped off the rack.

The dress Martina had intended to wear to the Autumn Festival hung from a brass hook on the inside of the door. A pale lilac in color, the dress was made of satin and had a fitted bodice with cap sleeves and a full skirt.

Sydney touched the fabric, thought of Victor, and turned away.

There were eight built-in drawers at the far wall, and here she could detect a police presence in the slight disorder of clothes. She wondered who'd drawn the assignment of going through Martina's lingerie.

Somehow, she couldn't imagine Dwight Grant sorting through all that silk and lace.

Whoever had done it hadn't missed as much as a stray hairpin; there was nothing in any of the drawers except for items of clothing. Then again, given the total lack of clutter in the room, it was entirely possible that there had been nothing for the police to find.

Considering that her own drawers were littered with loose buttons, safety pins, hair clips, mateless earrings, ticket stubs, sea shells, postcards, and the odd small keepsake, she found this neatness inexplicable. Where on earth had Martina tucked away the assorted flotsam and jetsam of life?

"Not," she said aloud, "in here."

In the bedroom proper, the only item that struck a familiar chord was the bowl full of matchbooks; although she didn't smoke, Sydney had a heavy glass ashtray full of matches she'd picked up around town.

She went to the shelf and took the fishbowl down, then walked over to the bed and dumped the matchbooks out. Among them she found tiny ten-match books from Disneyland, a box of white-tipped black wood matches from Benihana's, and a gold foil book from the Mirage in Las Vegas. The collection also included an assortment of matches from restaurants ranging from Elario's and La Valencia in La Jolla, to the Magic Castle and Spago's in Los Angeles, to more casual everyday places like Carlos Murphy's and the Black Angus.

There was even, curiously, a well-worn book from Hollywood Film Enterprises.

She stared absently at the matchbooks spread out on the bed for a minute or two, and then began scooping them up to return to the bowl. It occurred to her that if anyone came into the room right now, she'd have a very hard time explaining what in the hell she was doing.

Except maybe getting—or trying to get—a sense of who Martina had been . . .

She replaced the fishbowl on the shelf next to the gum ball machine. She noticed a saucer of pennies to the side and took one, inserting it in the slot. The gum ball the machine dispensed was candy apple red.

"Here's your chance, Dwight," she said, popping the gum into her mouth. "Arrest me for petty theft."

Chewing as she turned away, her eyes came to rest on the paperback on the nightstand. There was, she saw, a folded piece of paper at about the halfway point in the book, marking Martina's place.

She crossed the room once again and picked up the book, opening it and removing the makeshift bookmark. The paper had been folded into quarters, but even before she unfolded it, she knew what it was: a computer-generated notice from the San Diego Public Library system that a book Martina had requested was being held for her at the Central Branch on E Street downtown.

The title of the book was "How To Find Anyone, Anywhere, Anytime."

Written in pencil at the top right hand corner of the notice was the word Genealogy, and below that, a phone number.

In her Rolodex at the office, Sydney had a printed Directory of the Central Library, and she'd made enough phone inquiries over the years to recognize the prefix as the one the library used. Likewise, she'd spent hundreds of hours in the Genealogy Room—and the Newspaper Room—up on the second floor.

A journalism intern might indeed have reason to call the Genealogy extension, and requesting a book that would aid in tracking down a source or subject couldn't be considered at all unusual. Still, there was something about it that gave her pause.

If Martina's research had been an outgrowth of her job at the *Union-Tribune,* why not simply rely on the newspaper's files at the morgue? From what she knew of the newspaper's system, it was significantly better organized and cross-referenced.

Mulling it over, Sydney folded the library notice and replaced it in the book. She put the book cover side down on the nightstand and turned to leave.

Out in the hall, she heard at least two sets of footsteps, accompanied by the creak of leather and the jingle of keys.

"Cops," she said, and swallowed her gum.

Chapter Twenty-five

They were indeed cops, and there were two of them, but they weren't alone.

Between them, being supported and at times even carried, was none other than Randall Day. From fifteen feet away, Sydney could smell the alcohol fumes rolling off him, and see the rosy booze flush on his face. What wasn't immediately clear was whether he was groaning or crooning during the interval between hiccups.

Great Uncle Randall had tied one on.

Sydney backed up against the door to let them by when the cop nearest to her came to an abrupt stop.

"Sydney?"

Startled, she looked for the first time at the cop's face. Red hair and mustache, blue eyes, and the widest grin she'd ever seen. The mustache had been added since she'd last run into him—hadn't it been her sophomore year in college?—but it could only be . . .

Her eyes went to the gold nameplate above

his right shirt pocket. "Kevin Becker?"

"No one but," he said, and laughed. "What in the world are you doing here?"

"Working, of course."

"No shit. Hey—"

Uncle Randall had started to slump bonelessly to the floor, and Kevin and his partner manhandled him back onto his feet.

"Whoopsie," Randall Day said, and gave them all a beatific smile.

"We'd better get him squared away," the other deputy said, grunting under the strain of supporting half of the older man's not inconsiderable weight. Randall Day was as rotund as his sister Penelope was petite.

"Right." Kevin winked at her. "Stick around for a few minutes, I want to talk to you."

"Sure." She watched them make their way another two doors down the hall and into a room. Miss Penelope's brother began to sing an off-key rendition of "You Always Hurt the One You Love."

After a moment or two, she drifted nonchalantly after them, wanting a look at how far the police were going these days in the name of community relations. A lullabye seemed out of the question, but what about being tucked in by two of the county's finest?

When she got to the doorway, though, all she saw was Uncle Randall sprawled facedown on the bed. He was still singing, but the lyrics were muffled by the bedcovers. His right arm had fallen off the side of the bed, and he waved his hand back and forth as if conducting an orchestra only he could hear.

"Kevin?" she said, coming into the room.

Evidently the orchestra wasn't playing too loud, because Uncle Randall lifted his head from the pillows and looked over his shoulder at her. "Thank heavens you've come," he said, slurring his words just slightly.

Sydney noticed a flutter in the floor length drapes which indicated that the sliding glass door was open behind them. Obviously that was where Kevin and the other deputy had gone.

"I can't seem to turn myself over," Randall Day said. "If I was a tortoise and . . . and stranded on my shell, I'd be a goner, wouldn't I?"

She went to the old man's aid. It took a minute to coordinate the placement of his arms—perhaps he felt the bed moving because he kept grabbing handfuls of the quilt—and then she eased him over onto a nest of pillows so that he wasn't lying flat on his back.

"Bless you," he said, and closed his eyes.

She wrinkled her nose at the eighty-proof vapors. "Will you be all right now?"

One eye opened. "I should be."

"Good." She patted his hand, and looked at the drapes which were now billowing. She didn't understand how that kind of wind could be generated within the enclosed courtyard, but it was happening.

She took a step in that direction at the exact moment Great Uncle Randall grabbed her wrist.

"Don't go," he said. "Please."

His grip was surprisingly strong. "I just want to take a look—"

"Not there. You don't want to look there." A tremor passed through him and he came up off the pillows as if he'd received an electric jolt. At the same time he let go of her and covered his face with his hands.

"Easy," Sydney said. "Take it easy."

"Lock the door," he whispered urgently. "Hurry!"

She frowned, uncertain of what was going on. Was he afraid of something he'd seen, or was it the alcohol talking, or could it be something else entirely? In any case, his request gave her an opportunity to satisfy her curiosity on at least one score.

Once at the sliding door, she pushed aside the drape and saw Kevin and the other deputy standing across the courtyard near—she thought—the dressing room where she'd spent so many hours waiting on Tuesday night. She could hear the murmur of their voices, but couldn't make out what they were saying.

Judging by their relaxed body language, whatever they were talking about didn't appear to be of earth-shattering importance.

186

Sydney shook her head, perplexed at what had drawn them outside, and then turned to see Randall Day watching her with obvious consternation.

"Who *are* you?" he asked. He wiped the back of one trembling hand across his mouth.

"My name is Sydney Bryant, and I'm a private investigator."

"You are?"

"I am. Your sister hired me to look into Martina's death."

"Tina." The name wasn't as much spoken as sighed. He laid back on the pillows and folded his hands on his chest. "Poor Tina."

After her experience with Amanda Saxon, she wasn't too keen about the prospect of interviewing someone so clearly under the weather, self-induced or not.

But what the hell.

"Did you see anything that night?" she asked, returning to the bedside.

He blinked. "That night?"

"The night Martina was killed."

His expression seemed deliberately vacant, but if people's thoughts could be seen in a balloon over their heads the way a cartoon character's were, Sydney imagined Uncle Randall's would read: "Ask me about any night but that night, please, please, please."

"Oh," was all he said.

"Your room does open into the courtyard,

after all, and it stands to reason that you *might* have seen someone. Or heard something."

"They're out there," he said, disingenuously, "and we can't hear them."

So he wasn't as drunk as he appeared to be. Sydney smiled. "But I saw them."

He licked his lips and said nothing.

"Tina was your grandniece. Her mother tells me that she was very fond of you."

"A lovely girl," he said.

"A beautiful young woman."

"Yes." Another sigh, this one sounding as if it were sucking all of the air from his lungs out after it.

She let the silence grow until she saw his hands begin to fidget, and then asked, "When is the funeral?"

"Tomorrow," he said, and tightened his lips to keep them from quivering.

Sydney felt a sense of shame at asking an old man such an emotional question while he was under the influence, but her loyalty was with Martina, and if she had to use a slightly under-handed approach to get the answers she needed, she'd have to live with it.

"How old was she?" she asked, although she damned well knew, having heard over and over again the echo of the words she'd read, ... *female who appears to be her stated age of twenty-two* ...

"Twenty-two," Uncle Randall confirmed.

188

"Not out of college yet?"

He swallowed and wet his lips again. "This was her senior year."

"So much promise . . ."

"A lovely girl."

Feeling that she'd led the horse to water, she waited to see if he'd drink.

He did. "I saw her," he said in a hushed voice, "come out of her room."

Sydney felt her breath catch in her throat and her pulse quicken. *It can't be this easy,* a voice in her head warned, *it never is.*

"I don't think she saw me," he went on. "I hadn't turned the light on . . ."

In her mind, Sydney pictured the old man at the glass door, standing in the shadows of an early dusk.

"She went to the pool and reached down, to test the water I suppose."

She heard the deputies' voices become louder as they approached the door. She looked quickly in that direction and then back again at Randall Day, hoping that their return wouldn't spook him . . .

He appeared oblivious, the whites of his eyes prominent as he stared off into space. "And then she went back to her room," he said.

Sydney felt a heaviness in the pit of her stomach. "What?"

"I saw her go back to her room." His eyes shifted to meet hers, and now they were

189

hooded. "That was the last time I saw Tina."

The sliding glass door rumbled farther open, and Kevin Becker pushed aside the drape as they came in. "—could be rabid."

"Then call Animal Control," the other deputy said. "I'm not chasing after a god damned squirrel."

Numb with disappointment, Sydney sat on the side of the bed.

"I think maybe it was hurt." Kevin closed the screen and then the door.

The deputy snorted. "It didn't run like it was hurt. It ran like it had scored a line of cocaine."

"The poor thing was scared."

"Scared my ass. I'd have shot the mother—"

"Not shot," Uncle Randall said. "Not shot, or I would have heard."

Chapter Twenty-six

"Visit the Twilight Zone often?" Kevin Becker asked as they walked across the driveway toward his green and white patrol car, pausing momentarily as the second squad passed in front of them.

"I have resident status."

"Why doesn't that surprise me?" He went around to the driver's side, rested his elbows on the roof, and nodded in the direction of the house. "But what are you doing here of all places?"

"I told you. Working."

Kevin took off his dark glasses—there wasn't much sunlight anyway—rubbed the bridge of his nose and then squinted at her. "Doing what?"

"It has been a long time, hasn't it? I'm a private investigator."

"You? You're the wannabe?"

Sydney knew where he'd heard that. "I gather Dwight Grant hasn't much use for P.I.'s," she said archly, and forced a smile.

191

"P.I.'s, rookies, or wannabes. The man's an ex-Marine, and I don't think he's ever gotten it out of his blood. You've gotta look like a Marine, talk like a Marine, think like a Marine, and smell like a Marine to get on his good side."

"He has one?"

Kevin laughed. "Rumor is, anyway."

"Even if I saw it, I wouldn't believe it. And I'm *not* a wannabe."

"Hey, I hear you."

"Besides, I don't see him out here every day. As a matter of fact, I'm a little surprised that the place isn't crawling with deputies."

"That's not his style," Kevin said, and shrugged. "Once the crime scene's been thoroughly processed, he prefers to conduct the ongoing on his own turf. Having to answer questions in an interrogation room tends to upset most folk's equilibrium."

"That qualifies as an understatement. So you're here because . . ."

"Our Melancholy Baby in there showed up to give his statement this afternoon with a blood alcohol of point two oh or better."

"Or worse," she corrected.

"Right you are. We were dispatched to bring him safely home."

"Lovely duty."

"What can I say? Life isn't all hot pursuits

and take downs." He grinned again. "Although I think that squirrel might have been a BOLO . . ."

Sydney grinned back. BOLO was an acronym for Be On the Look Out for. "Funny, Becker. I think you may have missed your calling."

"Not in your life. Anyway," he said, "don't let Dwight get under your skin. It's nothing personal—"

"That's comforting."

"—he just likes to have his way, and the big brass shoved you down his throat."

She made a face. If insults, intentional oversights and misplaced statements were examples of how cooperative Grant was under direct orders from the boss, she could just imagine how things would be if the choice were left to him. "Wonderful."

"Exactly. He's catching a lot of heat on this one, and you make a convenient scapegoat. But so would any P.I. who got in his way."

"I feel better already," she said, making no attempt to disguise her sarcasm.

The cop in him caught it, but the old friend let it pass. "Good."

"By the way, do you know whether or not the department sent an evidence tech out to do a footprint cast up the hill there?"

Kevin turned to look in the direction she was pointing. "Footprints?"

193

"I'll take that as a no." She hadn't thought to check and see if the prints were still there on her way in this morning, but today at least she had her camera in the trunk of the Thunderbird.

And there was no time like the present. Particularly since the clouds had grown darker since she'd first noticed them, and seemed to be threatening rain.

"Mind if this rookie takes a look?" she asked, beginning to walk backward toward her rental car.

"Shit, no. I'll follow you."

Sydney sat on her heels at the side of the road and studied the soft dirt. Apparently it had sprinkled earlier and there were thousands of miniature craters in the soil. The footprints had been obliterated, either by the rain or other means.

"Do you see any signs they made casts?" She looked up at Kevin who was standing with his thumbs hooked inside his Sam Browne belt.

"Nope."

"Neither do I," she said, and frowned. She sifted dirt between her fingers; as fine-textured as it was, no wonder it hadn't held a print. "Damn it."

"Maybe the prints you saw had nothing to do with the case."

"Don't cheer me up." She straightened up and dusted off her hands.

"Come on now . . . it's not the end of the world."

"I wonder."

"Sydney, it isn't your fault. You reported it and that's all you could do."

"You know," she said, "this entire case has been one miscue after another. I've been a day late and a dollar short since the very start."

"It can't be that bad—"

"Yes it is." Frustration made her angry, and anger made her impatient. "I've been doing this for ten years, Kevin. I'm not a rookie. How could I have forgotten the little details—"

"Because they *are* little."

"But not insignificant. All I had to do was look for the note—"

"What note?"

"—and take a few photographs. Maybe nothing would have come of it, but it might have been important. Who knows what difference it might have made?"

"What note?" he asked again. "I reviewed the case file not more than an hour ago, and I don't remember anything about a note."

"It's in my statement. I amended my statement this morning to include it."

"You gave a statement?"

"Wait a minute. What are you saying? Now *my* statement is missing?"

"I don't know that anything's missing, Sydney, but I didn't find your statement in the file."

"Are you sure?"

"If I'd read your statement, I wouldn't have been surprised to see you, now would I?" His was the voice of reason. "And I'd have known you were the wannabe. I mean, the P.I."

Sydney stared at him in disbelief. What in the world was Dwight Grant up to? What could he possibly hope to gain by pulling her statement from the case file? Who the hell did he think he was?

The skies chose that moment to begin to rain. She looked up at the heavens and let the fat drops of water pelt her face.

"I think," she said, "I've got to think about all of this. I'm going home."

Chapter Twenty-seven

It was raining steadily by the time she reached the San Clemente Canyon exit off Interstate 5, and she lowered the window a couple of inches so that she could smell the fresh damp air. Southern California was in its fifth year of drought, but it seemed to her even longer since she'd whiled away a rainy afternoon.

There was something almost sinful about going home at two o'clock.

The carports at her apartment building were nearly empty, and when she parked, the Thunderbird was the only car in her row. She removed the keys from the ignition and then hesitated.

It wasn't like her, leaving the job this way. The obsessive side of her was inclined to at least go to the office and get a little paperwork done, but for once she managed to silence that voice.

She got out of the car and walked determinedly toward the wrought iron gate.

Sydney changed into what she thought of as
comfort clothes: a black sweatshirt, gray sweat-
pants, and black leg warmers. The sweatshirt
was a size too large and came down to mid-
thigh, but that was all the better.

She made a steaming mug of hot chocolate
and topped it off with a three-inch swirl of
whipped cream. Somehow that didn't seem to
be enough, so she tilted her head back and
squirted an equal measure of the whipped
cream directly into her mouth.

The doorbell rang.

It wasn't possible to swear with her mouth
full, so she didn't. She went through the small
dining room into the living room—stopping
briefly to put her mug of hot chocolate on the
coffee table—and then to the door.

She was still swallowing whipped cream as
she pulled the door open.

Mitch Travis was surveying the hallway, the
cop in him continually on the lookout for trouble, but he turned to face her with a smile, as
if work were the last thing on his mind. "Hello
stranger," he said.

"Mitch," she said, and thought, *Do I have
whipped cream on my mouth?*

If she did, it didn't seem to bother him. He stepped closer and leaned down to kiss her. He tasted, she thought, of rain.

"I wasn't sure you were home." His hazel eyes scanned the living room. "Or if you were alone."

"Of course I'm alone," she said, and frowned.

"That isn't your car parked in your space."

"Oh, that. It's a rental." She closed the front door and leaned against it, watching him as he took off his coat and hung it on a hook in the closet. Darkly handsome, dressed in chinos and a mint green turtleneck, with his black hair glistening from the rain, the man looked like he'd retail for a cool million.

"Day off?" she asked.

He smiled. "How'd you guess?"

"I'll never tell."

"I have ways," he said, taking a step toward her, "of making you talk."

Sydney stood her ground, not that she had much choice. Backed up against the door, she could feint to her right and get away, but she flat out didn't want to.

Mitch took her face in his hands and, after searching her eyes, kissed her again. And again.

Breathless after a minute or two, she pushed him gently, reluctantly away.

"God, I missed you," he said.

"If this is how you show it, maybe you

199

should miss me more often," she said, and then felt her color rise.

"I can arrange to show it more often," he said, and, brushing her hair out of the way, began to trail kisses along the side of her neck. "I can arrange to show it all night long."

"Don't—" she took a sudden breath as his teeth grazed her earlobe "—tempt me."

"Sydney . . ."

"Mitch . . . my hot chocolate's getting cold."

He laughed softly and released her. "One of these days, we're going to have to talk priorities."

She slipped by him and went to the couch to sit down before she got any weaker in the knees. "Damn," she said, reaching for the mug, "now look what you've done; my whipped cream's melted."

"I'll fix that." He started for the kitchen, but made a detour to the couch. Tilting her chin up, he bent down and brushed her lips with his. "I love you."

He was gone before Sydney could reply.

She sat Indian-style and pulled her leg warmers down to cover her bare feet. Mitch was at the other end of the couch, slowly shaking the can of Reddi-Whip in preparation for periodically refreshing her hot chocolate.

"You know," she said, "I don't think I ever truly appreciated the San Diego Police Department until I had to work with—make that try to *deal* with—the Sheriff's Department."

"Having problems?"

"A few." She held her mug out and watched with satisfaction as he filled it to the rim with Reddi-Whip. "Do you know Dwight Grant?"

"The jarhead? Yes, I know him."

She took a sip of tepid chocolate and had to lick whipped cream off her upper lip afterward. "What do you think of him?"

"He's a good cop."

"Oh." She should have known what the answer would be; there was a certain rivalry between departments, but cops were always looking out for each other, whether they worked together or not.

"Is he the one giving you problems?"

She sighed. "Yes." She told him as succinctly as possible what had been going on, including her suspicion that Grant was playing fast and loose with the truth.

When she finished, Mitch asked, "Do you want me to talk to him for you?"

"No! Absolutely not." She shook her head emphatically. "The last thing I need is for Dwight Grant to think I came running to you for help."

"He wouldn't think that."

201

"The hell he wouldn't."

"I could just mention that you're a friend, and let him take it from there."

"I can fight my own battles, Mitch."

"I know you can. You scare me sometimes, kid." He smiled and reached across to touch her nose. "Except when you miss a spot."

The incongruity of talking tough with whipped cream on her nose made her laugh. "You might have told me before now, Lieutenant."

"But you looked so cute." He took the mug out of her hand, put it and the Reddi-Whip on the coffee table, and turned her around so that she was resting against him, cradled in his arms. "I won't do anything you don't want me to do, but if you change your mind, all you have to do is say the word."

"Hmm." She closed her eyes.

"Or if you want, I'll kick his ass."

She found his hand, brought it to her face, and kissed the palm. "I don't think that will be necessary, but thanks for the offer . . ."

"You know I'd do anything in the world for you, Sydney. Anything."

He'd been saying that for months now, and she was beginning to believe that he really meant it, but what she wanted him to do at this minute was precisely what she was afraid of.

202

"Hold me," she said. "Just hold me."

His arms tightened around her.

Outside, a gust of wind blew the rain against the window.

Chapter Twenty-eight

Sydney suggested going out to dinner, but Mitch wanted to stay in.

"It'll give me a chance to show you what I can do in the kitchen," he said.

"I can hardly wait."

"That is—" he opened the refrigerator and freezer doors "—if you have any food in this place."

"I have lots of food." She yawned, still groggy from the nap she'd unexpectedly taken, and came to his side. "Look, there's frozen peas, and carrots, and . . . something else green."

"Not exactly nouvelle cuisine."

Sydney poked a finger at a roughly square package wrapped in aluminum foil. "This is probably some kind of meat."

"Circa when?"

"And this is—" she frowned at a dough-white, triangular object in a Zip-loc bag "—I don't know what in the hell this is."

"I can see that I'm going to have to do the

cooking when we're married." He guided her to the kitchen table and sat her in a chair.

"I haven't said I'll marry you."

"You will." He came within a millimeter of kissing her and then didn't, smiling at her when she moved marginally in his direction.

"Tease," she said.

"You betcha."

He went back to the refrigerator and began pulling things out seemingly at random and tossing them on the counter. "Why don't you tell me about this case you're working on while I'm fixing dinner?"

Sydney could think of better things to discuss, but much to her surprise she realized that she wanted his opinion on what she'd learned thus far. It didn't escape her notice that it used to be Ethan's opinions she sought, and she felt almost disloyal about that.

After last night, however, she thought it might be a while before she spoke with Ethan again.

"Well," she said, and took a deep breath. "If you insist . . ."

It took at least forty minutes to relate the week's events, and by the time she got around to Kevin Becker and the nonexistent footprints, Mitch was putting dinner on the table.

"And, like a spoiled brat," she concluded, "I picked my marbles up and came home."

"I'm glad you did."

205

She watched as he served her a conglomeration of stir-fried vegetables over a bed of brown rice. It looked and smelled delicious, and all at once she felt ravenous. "So am I."

Mitch sat across from her. "By the way, who is this Kevin Becker?"

"An old high school friend." She speared a carrot and practically inhaled it. She pointed her fork at her plate. "This is very, very good."

"I'm glad you like it. How close of a friend?"

"Mitch," she said, and laughed. "Why do you ask? Are you jealous?"

"To paraphrase a certain detective, the last thing I need is more competition."

"Kevin isn't competition."

"No?"

"No. We were friends. Becker, Bryant . . . he sat in front of me in maybe half of my classes, and we just hit it off. We're friends," she repeated.

"And nothing more?"

"Nothing more. He had a new girl every other week while we were in high school."

"And none of them were you?"

"No," she said absently, wondering where the celery in the stir-fry had come from. Then, noticing that Mitch looked skeptical, she added, "We got along too well to spoil things by going out."

"I see."

He didn't. "Listen, I heard Kevin profess undying love for too many girls to ever take him seriously as a romantic interest."

"And what about you?"

"Excuse me?"

"Who were you in love with?"

She put down her fork, folded her hands in her lap and said, "I respectfully refuse to answer on the grounds that it might incriminate me."

"That's what I thought."

"Mitch . . . why are we even talking about this? The point isn't Kevin . . . the point is, I had a rotten day. I'm getting nowhere so fast my nose is bleeding."

"All right," he said. "Let's talk murder."

"Let's talk suspects," she amended.

"Suspects, then. There were thirteen people in the house that night, and theoretically, they're all suspects. But I think you can safely eliminate the grandmother and the parents—"

"I haven't spoken with Jared Saxon yet."

"But he was with his wife. I would assume she would have noticed if he slipped out of the room and came back with bloodstains on his clothes."

Sydney inclined her head in agreement. "Okay, that leaves ten possible suspects."

"And you've talked to both of the brothers—"

"—who are more likely to have tried to kill each other than Martina."

"So they're not prime suspects."

"Except I think Owen Saxon could have done it. *Could* have."

Mitch frowned. "Convince me."

"He hasn't much in the way of moral fiber, for one thing. He hasn't shown a lot of emotion over his sister's death. He's a greedy little bugger." She paused briefly to organize her thoughts. "He strikes me as being very evasive, and claims to have no knowledge about anything that happened that night. And he lied about having given a statement to the police."

"That makes him a sorry excuse for a human being and a liar, not a killer."

"Maybe, but it was such a stupid, pointless lie, I'll keep him on my list."

"It's your list. What about the other brother?"

She considered for a moment and then shook her head. "I don't buy David as the killer."

"Why not?"

"Because he's the responsible one."

"Of the kids, you mean?"

"Right." She ticked them off on her fingers: "David is the responsible one, Owen is the selfish one, and Martina was the conscience of that family."

"Very interesting. Eliminate David and then you have nine."

"I'm glad you're keeping count. Okay. I talked to Randall Day this afternoon. He seemed to be

208

genuinely distressed by his grandniece's death, but if money is the motive—"

"It often is," Mitch observed.

"—then I don't think you can count old Uncle Randall out. He and Martina argued this past summer, and from what her mother says, she refused thereafter to give him a red cent."

"Did he have other sources of income?"

"I think so, but he's a gambler. Who knows what he might do if he got in over his head? And he'd been drinking today, but out of sorrow or remorse?"

Mitch smiled. "I admire your logic. You think like a cop."

"Thank you, I try." Sydney closed her eyes, trying to envision the rest of the faces. "Let's see, who else can we eliminate?"

"We're still holding at nine."

"Probaby the chauffeur; he wears a uniform and I don't think he'd have an opportunity to change if he got blood on it."

"Whoa, time out. Has the crime lab found any blood on anyone's clothes?"

"I am not privy to the crime lab's discoveries," she said pointedly. "You've forgotten the Gatekeeper, the Marine Corp's Dwight Grant."

"Ouch, a sore spot."

"Anyway, that brings us down to eight. Now, I haven't talked to her—I didn't even know she existed until today—but there's the cook, Margaret."

"It occurs to me," he said, "that any cook would be good with a knife."

"Only from the impression I got from David, Margaret's been with the family for years and must be as old as dirt. In her case, I am willing to bow to the FBI's wisdom that as people age, they are less likely to kill."

"I've seen their statistics, and I tend to agree. But age is in the eye of the beholder, and the younger the beholder, the more likely he is to over-estimate."

Sydney nodded, feeling he had a valid point. "David's in his mid-twenties."

"Exactly. A young pup like that could be off by ten or fifteen years. As a matter of fact, I have a nephew who thinks that *I'm* so old, he was amazed to hear that we had electricity way back in the prehistoric ages, when I was a boy."

"You did?" she asked with a laugh. "Regardless, I'm not going to consider her a suspect for now. If, when I talk to her, I notice any homicidal tendencies or special affinities for sharp objects, I may have to reconsider."

"It's your call," he said. "We're at seven and counting."

"Make it six. I think I can cross Mrs. Harrington off the list."

"Julie Harrington?"

"You know her?"

"Only slightly; we've been introduced once or twice. I know her husband better; he moves in very influential circles."

"Talking shit and wearing hip waders, no doubt."

Mitch raised his eyebrows. "So you're not a charter member of the Boyd Harrington fan club."

"I must have forgotten to mail in my dues. But he *is* still on my list."

"I'm impressed at the caliber of your suspects. The man will probably be named a Superior Court judge after the first of the year."

"That doesn't change my mind. Harrington acts like he has something to hide."

"Lawyers always do."

She realized that he was referring to Ethan as much as to Harrington, and that saddened her. Mitch and Ethan had been partners once, and had relied on each other for their very lives. Now, because of her, they hardly spoke. "Be nice," she said.

He didn't ask what she meant. "That brings us down to a tidy six. Anyone else you can eliminate?"

"No one yet."

"Of the six, I can account for three: Harrington's a suspect, Day's a suspect, and so is Owen Saxon. Who are the others?"

"Felice McDaniel," she said automatically. "She's David's fiancée."

"And how did she make the cut, if you'll excuse the expression?"

"I don't like her," Sydney said, enunciating each word precisely.

He drummed his fingers on the table. "Okay, it works for me. Who else?"

"The housekeeper, Edith Armstrong. I can't get over the feeling that the woman is seething inside about something."

"And she's the one who threw the infamous disappearing note out the window?"

"She's the one," she affirmed. "It may turn out to be nothing, but—"

"—you never know. So who's our final runner-up?"

"Chad Fuller. Martina's cousin on her mother's side. I haven't seen him yet either, but he was driving erratically after he left the house that night, and I get the impression that he's in and out of trouble."

"The black sheep of the family?"

"He could be," she agreed. "But then, with this family, trouble might mean he uses the wrong silverware at dinner."

"Well," Mitch said, "as long as it wasn't a knife . . ."

On that sober note, they fell silent.

* * *

At ten o'clock she walked with Mitch to the door. "Thanks for dinner. And for talking me through the case . . . it helped."

"Consider it a professional courtesy." He cupped her chin in his hand and kissed her.

A pleasant warmth radiated through her and she leaned into him. His hand on the small of her back provided another source of heat.

"I can stay if you want," he whispered in her ear.

Sydney moved her hands beneath his sweater and ran her fingers lightly over his bare back. It had been three years since they'd been lovers, but the feel of him seemed to have been burned into her soul.

She made herself pull away. "You'd better go."

Keeping his word to her, he didn't argue. "Good night, love."

Chapter Twenty-nine

Friday

In the morning, Sydney dressed in navy slacks and a red pullover, then went to her closet, looking for the only black dress she owned.

Martina Saxon's funeral services were to be held at one p.m.; however much she dreaded it, she had to attend.

She found the dress — a simple linen shift — still in the dry cleaner's plastic bag. The claim ticket pinned to the plastic gave a pick-up date in June.

She removed the claim ticket and threw it away; she didn't need any reminders of other funerals. June seemed both a long time ago and only yesterday . . .

After laying the dress out on her bed, she searched through the closet for her black pumps, and then went to the dresser to select pantyhose. In a dark mood, she decided to stay with basic black.

She took her change of clothes out to the rented Thunderbird—coincidentally also black—and then went back to the apartment to lock up.

The phone was ringing when she reached the door.

"It never fails," she muttered under her breath as she hurried to answer it. "Hello?"

For several seconds there was nothing. She held the phone away from her, intending to hang it up, but then heard a woman laughing.

"Who is this?" she demanded, and had the presence of mind to switch the answering machine from 'answer' to 'two-way' recording.

"I'm sorry," came the quiet reply, "I must have a wrong number."

The dial tone droned in her ear.

At the office, Sydney went straight to her desk with the intention of typing up interview notes from yesterday and the day before. She would also compose an interim report for Miss Penelope in the event that an opportunity arose to talk to her later this afternoon.

She rolled a green interview form into the typewriter and flexed her fingers, trying to decide where and with whom to start.

But the name that came to mind was Victor's, and no matter that she told herself she *had* to get some work done this morning, she knew what she really had to do was go and see him.

That is, if she could find him.

Two hours later, on her way back from a pool hall in Encinitas, she was stopped at the light at North Torrey Pines Boulevard and Carmel Valley Road when she spotted a van that resembled Victor's in the parking lot that served Torrey Pines State Beach.

Glancing behind her to make sure it was safe, she eased the Thunderbird over into the turn lane. When several minutes had passed without the light changing, she made an illegal left onto Carmel Valley Road. A quarter of a mile later, she made the sharp right at the entrance of the beach lot.

The gate was open and she drove in, slowing as she crossed a narrow bridge. The road widened beyond that, and she turned right at the east corner.

The van was straight ahead, parked at the farthest end of the lot. She lowered the window, listening for the sound of its engine. The pavement was still wet from yesterday's rain, though, and all that she heard was the angry hissing of her tires.

The van, a dark-colored Dodge, looked ominous to her in its isolation, and she thought inevitably of lost loves and suicide. And of the tortured look on Victor's face the last time she'd seen him.

She angled the Thunderbird to block the van and turned off the ignition.

The skies were partly cloudy and there was a brisk, cold wind blowing off the ocean. Perhaps a hundred yards away beyond the bluff, storm-driven waves battered the shore. Seagulls caught the wind and rode it, their cries sounding like an echo from a distant time.

Sydney got out and walked to the driver's side of the van. The windows were filmy and she had to shade her eyes to look inside.

There was nothing to see. Both the driver and passenger seats were empty. The van's floor was carpeted with a thick-piled green shag—a remnant of the seventies—and what she could see of it was mercifully uncluttered by dead bodies.

The out-stretched arm she'd braced herself for wasn't there, and she sent a silent "thank you" heaven-ward for that.

She tried the door, but it was locked. Making a quick circuit around the van, she determined that all of the doors were likewise secured. At the rear she took a few seconds to study the plate, but since she'd never had occasion or cause to memorize his license number, seeing this one wasn't of much help.

If this was Victor's van, where was he?

The beach, she thought, and fought back images of a body being washed ashore.

Despite the weather—or because of it?—there were a few hearty souls who were drawn to the beach. Here, without the barrier of the bluff and roadway above, the wind was stinging. It blew her hair across her face and whistled icily in her ears.

She hadn't gone more than a hundred yards when she decided that she wasn't dressed for this. Although she'd pulled the sleeves of her pullover to cover her hands and wrapped her arms around her midriff, she began to shiver. The damp spray from the breaking waves made the cold intolerable.

"Bad idea," she said, and clenched her teeth to keep them from chattering.

She turned to go back and saw a familiar ungainly figure coming toward her.

Relief made her almost giddy, and she ran in his direction, ignoring the wet sand that invaded her shoes.

"Victor!" she yelled.

Thirty feet away, he didn't seem to hear her. He walked with his head down, kicking at the rocks that seemed to breed on this beach. He had on a yellow windbreaker, but it wasn't

218

zipped up, and it billowed out behind him, a land-locked sail.

"Victor!" She planted herself in front of him to block his way.

He looked up. The dampness had frizzled his perm beyond repair. His face was red and wind-burned, his eyes tearing. He wiped the back of his hand under his runny nose.

She'd never seen him look better.

"What are you doing here?" he asked.

"Looking for you. Victor, you'll freeze to death." She reached around him and grabbed the coat tails of the windbreaker, bringing them together in the front. The zipper wanted to stick, but she forced it halfway up.

As if he were a child, Victor just stood there, his arms limp at his sides, suffering the indignity of being dressed by his mother without complaint.

"Come on," she said. When he didn't move, she grabbed the front of his jacket and pulled.

"Get in the car," she said, holding the door open for him.

This time he complied, although he narrowly missed hitting his head on the roof. The Thunderbird had more leg room than her Mustang, but even so, his bended knees reached the top of the dash.

Sydney slammed the door and went around to

the other side. Once inside, she started the car and turned on the heater full blast.

"Bless you, Henry Ford," she said a minute later as she began to thaw. "Bless you and all the little Fords."

Out of the corner of her eye, she saw Victor smile. She reached over and rested her hand on his. "So . . . Victor . . . a nice day for a walk on the beach?"

He gave her a sideways glance and then laughed. "Not particularly, no."

"What were you doing out there?"

"Just thinking."

His voice sounded normal to her; the strange hollowness was gone. "Me too. I've been thinking about you, and how you're going to get through today."

"The funeral, you mean."

"Yes." She hesitated. "Are you planning to go?"

"I can't."

It was the answer she expected, and she nodded to show she understood. "Victor . . . I want to try again and explain to you why I took this job."

"You don't owe me an explanation. If anything, I owe you one."

"Oh, I don't think so."

"But I do. I had no business acting that way.

It's just . . ." His words trailed off and he sighed.

Their eyes met and she saw healing in his. *Tell it in your own time,* she thought. *When you're ready, and not until.*

Evidently he was ready now. "These past few months, I've fancied myself in love with Martina, and imagined that one day she might love me. Reality didn't exist in the world I created. I'll never know whether she would have laughed in my face when and if I worked up enough courage to ask her out—"

Knowing how difficult this must be for him, she hadn't wanted to interrupt, but she couldn't let that pass. "I don't think she'd have laughed, Victor."

"No one will ever know, and I think that's for the best."

She couldn't argue with that.

"What I'm trying to say," he continued, "is that I idealized Martina, and by doing that, I kept her at a safe distance. I saw her and spoke to her, but there was always that space between us. The girl I daydreamed about and the girl I saw at work . . . weren't the same at all."

"But by coming to me," she said, "weren't you trying to move beyond daydreams?"

"Was I, really? Would I have ever approached her? I can't say. Or was I merely looking for a way to enhance the dream? I don't know."

221

It wasn't for her to say either.

"And that's why I don't want to hear the details, ever. Martina is dead in *that* world —" he looked briefly out the window, where the rain had resumed, and then touched a finger to his temple "— but not this one."

Chapter Thirty

As if by divine arrangement, the rain stopped for the duration of the graveside service. The clouds hovered close overhead, muddy gray and swirling in the wind.

Standing apart from the family members gathered, Sydney looked from face to face as the minister recited the 23rd Psalm.

"The Lord is my shepherd; I shall not want."

Penelope Day Saxon had aged in the days since her granddaughter's death. The black crepe dress she wore seemed ill-fitted, and she appeared fragile, even brittle, as though a touch would shatter her into a million pieces, beyond anyone's ability to repair.

"He maketh me to lie down in green pastures: he leadeth me beside the still waters."

Jared Saxon stood to her right, a slightly bemused expression on his face, as if he hadn't quite figured out what he was doing here. Hands clasped behind his back at parade rest, he had yet to look at his youngest child's casket.

"He restoreth my soul: he leadeth me in the path of righteousness for his name's sake."

Amanda Saxon was at her husband's side. Dark glasses hid her eyes but not the tears which streamed unchecked down her face. Even at a distance, Sydney could see her tremble and she wondered why Jared Saxon appeared unaware of his wife's emotional state.

"Yea, though I walk through the valley of the shadow of death, I will fear no evil: for thou art with me; thy rod and staff they comfort me."

A step behind Amanda, Owen Saxon shifted from foot to foot, occasionally glancing over his shoulder as though looking for someone among the mourners. But then he placed his hand on his mother's shoulder and leaned forward to whisper in her ear.

"Thou preparest a table before me in the presence of mine enemies: thou anointest my head with oil; my cup runneth over."

Standing perhaps six feet away from the rest of his family, David Saxon comforted Felice McDaniel, both arms around her. His face twitched almost continually, and Sydney thought it was to keep from crying.

Bereavement very much became Felice . . . stylish in a black suit with a pleated skirt and burgundy blouse, she also wore a tiny hat with a delicate black veil. One black-gloved hand rested against her slender throat.

"Surely goodness and mercy shall follow me all the days of my life: and I will dwell in the house of the Lord for ever."

To Miss Penelope's left, Randall Day showed the effects of the day after in the dark circles under his eyes and the puffiness of his face. He rocked on his heels gingerly, presumably with the aim of protecting those brain cells he hadn't lost to alcohol.

A female soloist with a clear, fresh voice began to sing, accompanied by a flute:

"Amazing grace, how sweet the sound, that saved a wretch like me . . ."

A young man Sydney hadn't met stood beside Uncle Randall. Perhaps five foot ten and stocky, his dark hair was cut so short that it was not much more than bristle, allowing the white of his scalp to show through.

Chad Fuller, she thought.

Presumably out of deference to his grandmother, he had dressed in a gray suit which he'd accessorized with black paratrooper boots.

"I once was lost, but now I'm found . . ."

Catching her watching him, the young man she assumed to be Martina's cousin glared at her.

A ferocious little thug, she thought, and not

the brightest off-shoot of the family tree. Talking with this one might prove interesting.

Several paces back, Boyd and Julie Harrington stood with other friends of the family. The future judge had his head lowered, his hands clasped respectfully in front of him. His wife, curiously, had turned a shoulder to him and was facing away.

"Was blind but now I see . . ."

Sydney recognized, as well, several young men who Martina had dated, none of whom were visibly grieving. One nautically-attired Lothario was actually making the rounds, moving through the crowd and mingling as if this were a rather morbid yard party. Another winked at her when their eyes met.

Standing on a rise to the far left was Dwight Grant and a uniformed deputy. She stared at Grant, willing him to look at her, but he didn't. He pointed, instead, at the road that circled through the cemetery, the road now lined with dozens of limousines.

Considering that his purpose in attending the funeral was the same as hers, he didn't appear to be much interested in the proceedings.

A gust of wind carried off the last notes from the flute, and again the minister stepped forward.

"The loss of a child," he said with authority, "is a terrible burden."

Sydney glanced again at Amanda Saxon, who was now holding a handkerchief to her mouth. Lines had appeared around her eyes as she fought to maintain her composure, and her brow was deeply furrowed.

"But in His wisdom, the Lord never gives us more than we can bear . . ."

Amanda's pain was raw and still bleeding, and its intensity forced Sydney to look away. She closed her eyes and prayed for the service to end.

". . . and we are reminded that in the midst of life we are in death."

From a long way off, a siren sounded and she squeezed her eyelids closed even tighter. Misery, she thought, at any time of the day or night, someone finds misery.

"Earth to earth," the minister intoned, "ashes to ashes, dust to dust . . ."

There was a murmur of voice, a startled cry, and a sound—a kind of whisper—that she couldn't identify. Sydney felt the light as she opened her eyes, blinked several times, and then saw that someone had slumped to the ground in a dead faint.

It was not, however, Amanda Saxon who'd collapsed, but her husband.

Chapter Thirty-one

Sydney caught up to Dwight Grant as he reached an unmarked beige sedan, parked behind the squad car and in front of the six motorcycles that had escorted the funeral procession.

She knew better than to grab his or any policeman's arm, and instead darted around him, positioning herself between him and the door. "Lieutenant . . . can I talk to you for a minute?"

Grant squinted at her as if he couldn't believe his eyes. "You again."

"And again and again and again. I'm not going to go away."

"You know," he said, and took his time looking her up and down, "if you applied yourself and really put your mind to it, you could probably make someone a pretty good little secretary."

She stared at him.

"If you showed your legs more often, I

228

wouldn't mind giving you dictation myself."

"Be still my heart."

Grant laughed, but it wasn't a friendly sound. "Not interested, huh?"

"Not even remotely. All I want from you is a few answers."

"Really. Well, that doesn't sound too difficult. Tell you what, hon. You come down to my office, say about five o'clock? And I'll have a few answers for you, to questions you haven't even thought of."

"I'm serious—"

"And so am I."

Sydney hesitated, trying to read him. He wanted, she thought, to incite her to anger, and suggestiveness was his weapon of choice. Maybe he believed that by coming on to her he could scare her away.

Guess again, she thought.

"Tell you what, hon," she said, fighting fire with fire and turning his own words against him, "let's don't and say we did."

This time when he laughed, he sounded amused. "Damn, but you're annoying. Why don't you just slap my face and walk off in a huff?"

"Because I won't get any answers that way. Now, can we talk?"

He looked around. People were leaving and there was a steady flow of traffic driving by, as well as the car doors being slammed and engines revved. Besides the noise, it had started to sprinkle again.

"Get in the car, Miss Bryant," he said. "We'll talk there."

To his credit, Dwight Grant remained silent as she listed what she considered lapses in the cooperation Penelope Day Saxon had been promised by his superiors.

"I can appreciate that this is a sensitive case," she said, "and I certainly understand that you might rightfully resent what you consider to be interference in your handling of it—"

"Consider to be!"

"But the fact remains that I'm not asking for any more than what was promised."

Grant frowned. "That's all well and good, but I'll be damned if I know what you're fussing about. I let you review the case file—"

"An incomplete case file," she said. "I know that there were statements missing."

"Missing," he said, and grunted his displeasure. "This comes as news to me."

"Does it? Tell me, how many statements has your office taken so far?"

"I haven't been counting."

That was a non-answer, and she wasn't about to let him off the hook that easy. "Then I'll count for you. Who have you talked to?"

"Look, Miss Bryant—"

"Obviously by now you've spoken to most if not all of the family."

His smile dripped sarcasm. "Obviously."

"Miss Penelope?" At his grudging nod, she continued naming names: "Jared Saxon? Amanda Saxon? David Saxon? Owen?"

"All of them, sure."

"Felice McDaniel?"

"Yes, just this morning in fact. And the others, that drunk of an uncle, and the punk, what's-his-name? Fuller. And before you bust my chops about it, we've talked to all of the household help, including a couple of maids who weren't even there that night."

"Boyd Harrington?" she persisted. "Julie Harrington?"

"I know this may come as a shock to you, but the taxes you pay don't all go to waste. We do know how to do our jobs."

"Can I take that as a yes? You have statements from the Harringtons?"

"Yes," he sighed, "we have statements from the Harringtons."

"So . . . you've talked to all those people, but there were only *three* statements in the case file when I saw it yesterday," she said, and held up the requisite number of fingers as a visual aid. "Three."

231

Grant shrugged. "The others were probably still being transcribed."

"Just how gullible do you think I am, Lieutenant?"

"The jury's still out, Miss Bryant."

She gave him a quick hard smile. "Fine. While we're waiting for a verdict, why don't you make a note to yourself to have copies made of the statements that have been transcribed? Then stick them—"

"Careful."

"—in a manila envelope and write my name on it. I'll pick them up later this afternoon."

He made a show of thinking it over, scratching his head and frowning before slowly nodding. "I guess I could arrange that."

"And while you're at it, maybe you wouldn't mind giving me a list of the items you removed from Martina's bedroom and any other place in the house."

"Don't want much, do you?" he asked, raising his bushy eyebrows.

"Not really."

"Shit."

"And—"

"And? And what! You're not finished?"

"And I'd really appreciate it if I could review any pertinent crime lab reports. Bloodstain analysis and that kind of thing."

For a moment he said nothing, drumming his

232

fingers on the steering wheel. Then he turned his head away, trying to hide a smile.

When he looked back at her a few seconds later, his expression was cool and detached. "Well, sweetheart, I don't know that I can give you everything on your wish list, as much as I'm dying to earn your appreciation, but I'll see what I can do."

Stunned that he hadn't refused her last request outright, she said, "That's all I ask."

"Only make it tomorrow, okay? I have a few previous engagements this afternoon."

Because the rain had resumed in earnest, Dwight Grant drove her to where her car was parked off the side of the road.

"Thanks," she said, "for everything."

Dwight Grant nodded but didn't answer. Neither did he meet her eyes.

Chapter Thirty-two

At Miss Penelope's insistence, Sydney went to Villa Saxon for the private gathering of friends and family, in memory of Martina.

Funerals generally robbed her of appetite, but the same was not true of everyone; there were tables laden with food, and at least two bars manned by discreet tuxedoed bartenders who formed a duet popping champagne corks.

As a latecomer, she had no way of knowing how solemn the gathering had been in the beginning, but when she arrived, the atmosphere, if not festive, was at least light-hearted. There was even, she noted, a string quartet playing in the background.

"Take your coat?" Edith Armstrong asked, a dour look on her face.

"Edith, can I talk to you?"

"I suppose you can."

"Somewhere private?" Across the room, laughter erupted among a group of middle-aged men in three-piece suits. "And quiet?"

The housekeeper folded Sydney's coat over her arm. "Follow me."

They made their way through the crowded living room into the even more crowded hallway. Looking at faces, Sydney didn't recognize very many as having been at the service. Where had they come from? she wondered.

The kitchen, which she'd assumed was their destination, was swarming with white-uniformed servants. At the stove, a tiny old woman whose back was twisted from scoliosis stood on a wooden stool so that she could stir mulled cider in an enormous copper pot.

Sydney tapped the housekeeper on the shoulder. "Is that Margaret?"

Edith glanced in the direction she was pointing. "And who else would it be? Come on, will you . . . I can't be away too long."

A door she hadn't noticed before led off to the left of the kitchen into a small sitting room. Along the outside wall, dormer windows overlooked the lush front gardens and sparkling fountains. Sydney was immediately taken with the serenity of the view.

But the view clearly wasn't the center of interest in this room. Four overstuffed chairs were arranged in a semicircle in front of a color television set. The TV was on but there was no sound.

"This is where we take our breaks," Edith

said, and plunked herself down, sinking into the cushions with unmistakable relief.

Sydney wasn't sure she'd ever get out of the chair if she sat down, so she perched on the arm instead. "Edith, I have a few questions—"

"More questions? Do they pay you by the one?"

"Not exactly. But the other day, we were interrupted by Mr. Harrington before I got to the question that most interests me."

"Isn't that the way," the housekeeper said wonderingly. "Isn't that just the way."

"I don't know if you've heard or not, but on Tuesday night, when Martina was killed, I was parked up there on the hill."

"I did hear something of the sort." Her eyes had strayed to the television screen, where an elegant dance number from a Fred Astaire movie promoted a week of coming attractions.

"From where I was parked, I could see everyone as they left, Edith."

"I suppose you did. Will you look at that, I swear old Fred's a treasure. Elegant, elegant man."

Sydney wondered if the housekeeper's seeming distraction was real or calculated. There was one way to find out. "As you drove by, I saw you throw a crumpled piece of paper out of the car window."

At first there was no reaction, and then the

236

woman turned to Sydney, a puzzled look in her slate gray eyes. "Did I? I don't remember."

"The police have been looking for the note—"

"Oh, I don't think it was a note, in the way that you mean."

"Excuse me?"

"Not as in correspondence, a note from someone to me, or vice versa."

"No?"

"I mean, I don't remember exactly, but knowing myself as I do, I can tell you that I wouldn't throw anything personal away."

"What else could it have been?"

Edith puffed her cheeks out as she thought, then released her breath in a rush. "Well. You have me at a disadvantage. It's embarrassing to be caught littering on the grounds, but then to have to admit I don't know what I threw out. It might have been an old grocery list or a reminder to myself to pay a bill—"

"Maybe I can help you to remember," she interrupted. "The interior light was on in your car, and you had an angry expression on your face."

Edith Armstrong made a sound and it took Sydney a few seconds to realize the housekeeper was laughing.

"I trust it won't shock you to learn that the *angry* expression you saw is habitual with me. When I was a child, adults were always asking me what I was mad about . . . not to scowl so or my face would freeze that way . . . and it appears they were right."

"But you are angry, aren't you Edith?"

She blinked slowly, deliberately. "I'm not sure I should answer that."

"What was it you threw away? It wasn't a grocery list, was it?"

"I don't recall."

"Someone had written you a note that made you angry. Whether you were reading it for the first time or taking another look, it infuriated you—"

"Infuriate is a very strong word," Edith demurred.

"But it's the right word, isn't it? What made you angry that night? Who wrote the note?"

"I know the police haven't found it," the housekeeper said shrewdly, "or *they* would have been around again to ask me about it."

Skirting the edge of truth, Sydney responded, "They're still looking."

"Are they? I wish them luck. After the rain we've had lately, I'd be surprised if they'd find more than a sodden wad of paper."

"Then again, I could be wrong about them looking . . . they might have already found it. They might be analyzing the handwriting, or the paper or the ink. I know they'll test for fingerprints."

Again that deliberate blink. "All that trouble over a grocery list?"

Sydney allowed herself a faint smile. "All the trouble, Edith, is about murder."

"I didn't kill her."

"I wasn't implying that you had."

"Weren't you?"

"No." And strangely enough, considering that last night she'd considered Edith Armstrong a viable suspect, that was the truth. "But I think you do know something about Martina's death."

Edith sat perfectly still, waiting, Sydney thought, for her to tip her hand.

Meeting that cool gaze, she was struck by the fact that Edith always had a measured response for any occasion. Except . . . except she remembered how affronted the woman had been when Harrington had chastised her for being late with tea, implying—or so it must have seemed to her—that she was remiss in her duties.

What that suggested was that Edith took an inordinate pride in her position in the household.

"If anyone knows how Miss Penelope is feeling, I do. I've worked in this house, for this family—"

Sydney thought it was worth a try. "I would imagine after all the years you've worked for Miss Penelope, that you *know* this family as well as anyone could . . ."

"Better," Edith affirmed. "After twenty-seven years, much better."

"Then you must have a feel for what's been going on."

"That's true."

Sydney hesitated, sensing that Edith Armstrong could be persuaded to reveal what she knew, and yet fearing that the wrong word might turn her off.

"You were fond of Martina," she said, more statement than question.

"Of the three children, she was my favorite."

"And it was obvious to me yesterday that you care for Amanda's welfare."

"I hate to see a decent woman suffer," Edith said simply. "If there was anything I could do to help her, I would."

"You know what would help her."

"What I know is what you're doing, Miss Bryant. You're pussy-footing around here, trying to get me to say more than I should—"

"Not more. Just enough."

"If I tell you enough, as you say, it won't be the end of it. Reporters will swoop down like a colony of ravenous locusts, and by the time they're through, there'll be nothing left for my retirement."

"What? I don't under—"

A spark of animation showed in Edith's eyes. "I'm writing a book about the Saxons, all that

240

I've seen in twenty-seven years. If I were foolish enough to go telling their secrets out of turn, it'd be the same as cutting my own throat."

"But—"

"Of course, I am going to wait until Miss Penelope passes over, out of respect. That is, if she doesn't outlive me."

Assimilating this new development, Sydney couldn't deny it had a certain twisted logic. If nothing else, it explained the housekeeper's secretiveness.

"Oh, the things I've seen, you wouldn't believe. From Master Jared's first kiss to young David and his bride-to-be skinny-dipping in the moonlight."

"I'm sure it's fascinating," Sydney said absently, and tried to punt: "But using what you know to help to find Martina's killer would make what you know more valuable, not less."

"Of course you'd say that. Wasn't it a reporter who hired you to watch her?"

"He wasn't after a story on the Saxon family, Edith. He wanted to know more about Martina because he'd fallen in love with her."

"Oh," she said. "I hadn't heard that."

The problem with eavesdropping, Sydney thought, was you so seldom got the whole story.

"Well, then, if you're not working with that reporter fellow, I guess I can tell you a thing or two. You can draw your own conclusions."

241

"Yes?"

"The note you're so interested in? The fine and upright Mr. Harrington wrote it, but not to me. I saw him slip it under Martina's plate at the table as they were coming in to dinner, and I took it."

"What did it say?"

"He asked her to meet him at nine o'clock at the Captain's Tower."

Sydney shook her head. "Where?"

"It's an observation deck at The Tides, where the Festival was being held."

"I see."

"I didn't have a chance to read it until later, of course, and then—" she shrugged "—I threw it away like the trash it was."

"To your knowledge, was Martina involved with Boyd Harrington?"

"I don't know positively that she was, but I'd heard her on the phone to his office, asking for him, and he's called here many, many times."

"Did you ever see them alone together?"

"Catch them kissing, you mean?"

"Or whatever."

"No, but a few months ago, I saw him coming out of her room. It was on a Sunday, I remember."

"Did he see you?"

Edith shook her head. "The hallway can be dark, and it was late afternoon. I stepped back

242

in the shadows—if he'd come in my direction he would have seen me—but he went the long way around."

"That's interesting. Did you—"

The clamorous sound of breaking glass in the kitchen brought Edith abruptly to her feet. "Sorry, but I have to get back."

Having gotten much more than she'd anticipated, Sydney merely nodded.

Chapter Thirty-three

Sydney went in search of Boyd Harrington.

In the time she'd spent with Edith, the crowd had thinned, but there were still enough people to make looking for any one person difficult. Someone handed her a glass of champagne as she wandered through the living room, and she sipped it judiciously.

As savvy as Harrington was, she'd need her wits about her when she confronted him.

If she confronted him; the constantly shifting flow of people from room to room and clique to clique might keep her perpetually a step behind.

"Have you seen Boyd?" she asked a distinguished-looking man who had taken up a solitary position by the fireplace. Six empty glasses were lined up on the mantel, the ice cubes in them at varying degrees of melting, and he held an identical glass in his hand.

"Harrington? No, but Julie was here a few minutes ago. Left to take an aspirin."

Having observed that some wives seemed to come equipped with husband-sensing radar, Sydney thought that finding Julie Harrington was an acceptable substitute. "Which way did she go?"

The man pointed with the stem of his pipe toward the courtyard.

Sydney nodded her thanks, put her champagne glass on the mantel, and returned to the fray.

There was only a trio of people in the courtyard proper, and Julie Harrington wasn't among them.

Since one was the pseudo-yachtsman she'd noticed circulating at the funeral—now he'd removed his shoes and socks, rolled up his cuffs and was dangling his feet in the pool—she decided against asking if they'd seen either Harrington.

Across the way, though, beyond the pool, a glass door had been propped open. She could hear voices coming from inside, and headed in that direction.

She reached the door at the same instant as Felice McDaniel.

Sans veil, Felice's dark hair formed a sleek cap, except for the three perfect curls that might well have been glued to her right cheek. She'd traded her mourning outfit for an English riding habit, complete with jodhpurs, black boots, and a wicked looking crop.

"Felice," she said, taken aback. "You're going riding?" She censored 'actually' and 'at a time like this' from the question.

"I'm sorry, do I know you? Oh . . . yes. You're the private detective. Miss . . ."

"Bryant. Do you have a few minutes? I'd like to talk to you."

"I can't." Felice smiled and touched Sydney's wrist lightly; her fingers were ice cold. "David's waiting at the stables."

"One minute," Sydney bargained. "Sixty seconds. That's all I'm asking."

"I'm already late, sorry."

And she was off. Sydney watched her dash across the courtyard, her boots creating a hurried echo in the enclosed space. The yachtsman waved and called to her, but she never lost a step.

"You can run," she said under her breath, "but you can't hide."

When she found Julie Harrington in a guest lounge, the woman was standing in front of a mirror staring into her own eyes. Her purse had been up-ended onto the marble counter. Its contents were spread out haphazardly; a loose powder compact had fallen to the floor, and a lipstick had rolled into the sink.

A small container of aspirin sat opened and empty among the mess.

"Mrs. Harrington?"

Julie Harrington responded by closing her eyes. She gripped the edge of the counter with both hands and leaned heavily against it.

"Mrs. Harrington, I'm a private investigator—"

"Look what I've done," Mrs. Harrington said, and grabbed the lipstick from the sink. "Careless of me."

Sydney took a step closer and in the mirror saw the panicked look in the woman's eyes.

"Harder every year," she said and began to apply her lipstick. "The cosmetic companies shouldn't sell make-up to women of an age. They should be honest and tell us that it won't do any good."

"You look fine."

"They ought to tell you how ridiculous you'll look." She'd drawn her mouth too broadly, accentuating the bow of her upper lip. "Ridiculous and dated and desperate. Every year, it gets harder and takes longer. And the girls get younger."

"Mrs. Harrington," she said carefully, "would you like to sit down?"

"Sit down?" After picking the powder puff

off the floor, she began dusting her face, oblivious to the fine film of powder that spilled onto her dress.

"Please?"

"There," Julie Harrington said, and nodded at her reflection. "All done."

"I think you'd feel better if you sat down."

She tossed the lipstick and powder puff in her bag, which she then held at the edge of the counter as she swept the other items inside. Then she turned so that she was facing Sydney.

"Am I beautiful?"

"Yes." Sydney felt dangerously out of her league here, but wasn't sure what she should do. "Come and sit down with me, Mrs. Harrington."

"My scarf," the older woman said, both hands going to her throat, her purse dropping unheeded to the floor where it burst open again. "Where's my scarf?"

"Come on," Sydney coaxed. "I'll help you look for it."

"It *was* here."

"You sit down, and I'll find it for you. Scout's honor."

"All right. Thank you."

Sydney ushered Julie Harrington toward the red plush divan in a back corner of the lounge. Along the way, she saw the missing scarf; it had been rolled up into a ball and thrown toward a wicker waste basket.

She retrieved it and placed it in Mrs. Harrington's eager hands.

"Thank you *so* much. You're very kind." She ran her fingers over the material repeatedly, smoothing out the wrinkles, and when she glanced up, the fear had disappeared from her eyes. "Did you say, dear, that you're a private investigator?"

"Yes."

"Do you know my husband?"

A moment ago Sydney would have sworn that Julie Harrington was on the brink of an emotional abyss. The switch from that near-psychotic episode to polite conversation made her somewhat uneasy, and she settled for a nod.

"Of course, I know who you are. Penelope hired you. That's right, isn't it?"

"Yes, it is." She watched, fascinated, as Julie Harrington arranged the scarf stylishly around her neck, then tied a series of knots so neatly there wasn't more than a shade's difference in size between them. And this without a mirror.

"We were here that evening, you know." Mrs. Harrington laughed suddenly, shrilly. "How foolish of me. Of course you know."

"Mrs. Harrington—"

"I insist you call me Julie. After witnessing my . . . my little fit of hysterics . . . surely there's no need for formalities."

"Julie, then. Do you mind if I ask what you remember about that night?"

"What I remember." She began twisting her engagement and wedding rings around her finger. "Well, I don't remember bringing along that knife."

Sydney felt her breath catch in her throat, but before she could respond, Julie Harrington laughed again.

"Oh, I'm only kidding," she said. "A little joke. Inappropriate perhaps, but this whole thing is so awful . . . it's either laugh or cry."

Or go crazy, Sydney thought.

"To be honest, I've had a hard time keeping my mind off what happened. Of course, it makes it harder that we've known Martina since she was six or seven. I've watched her change from a little girl with scabs on her knees into a lovely young lady."

A lovely young lady your husband was seeing on the side?

Julie continued to twist her rings; a red mark appeared beneath them. "Boyd was particularly close to her. I can remember how she'd come running when she heard his voice, and throw herself into his arms."

"Do you have children?" It was the only thing she could think to ask.

"No. I had scarlet fever when I was young. The doctors said my heart wouldn't bear it."

How was her heart bearing up now?

"On Tuesday," Julie Harrington said almost dreamily, "Boyd said he had something private to discuss with Martina. He wouldn't tell me what."

Sydney tried to gird herself to ask the questions she needed to ask, but as she strung the words together in her mind, Julie went on:

"When he came out of the library, I accused him of all sorts of horrible things. He wouldn't answer me, didn't say a word, and I slapped him." She looked down at her hands, which lay open, palms upward, on her lap. "My diamond cut him on the face, just a scratch really, although it wouldn't stop oozing blood, but I felt as if he'd plunged a knife into my heart with his silence . . ."

"The library?"

"Yes. They'd gone in there to talk."

Sydney frowned. "And Martina? Was she there when you argued?"

"Yes, and I feel terrible about that. If you could have seen the look on her face . . ."

"When was this?"

"Right before dinner."

That would explain Amanda's impression that her daughter had been sad at dinner, and it certainly explained the scratch on Harrington's face, but what about the note Edith had intercepted?

"I felt terrible about the whole affair," Julie continued. "I wanted to go to her and apologize, but Boyd wouldn't let me."

That could be interpreted in more than one way. No man relishes the prospect of his wife confronting his mistress.

If she *was* his mistress.

"So you didn't see or talk to her after dinner?" Sydney asked.

"No. Boyd felt I needed calming down. He took me in the living room and gave me a brandy. It helped; a little later when we left, I was . . . quite calm."

"He stayed with you that entire time?"

"Yes. Well, except for a minute or two, when he went to wash the blood off."

A minute or two.

"Owen came in about that time, though, so I was never alone."

Sydney reassessed Julie Harrington who, despite her earlier hysteria, had the presence of mind to offer an alibi for herself.

And, it seemed, for her husband.

Chapter Thirty-four

After leaving Julie Harrington, Sydney headed for the car to get her slacks and sweater, intending to change clothes before she went to look for David and Felice at the stables.

Somehow she'd lost track of the time, and was surprised to find it near sunset.

She was also surprised to come upon Boyd Harrington and Randall Day standing by the fountain nearest the front terrace. Harrington frowned when he noticed her—hurt my feelings, she thought—and glanced away.

Feeling contrary, she took that as an invitation, and walked toward them.

"—doesn't mature for a couple of weeks," Uncle Randall was saying, "so you can understand my reluctance to tap into it now. Penalties, you know."

"I can't promise, Randall, but call my office on Monday and I'll see what I can do."

"Oh that's splendid." His expression was one of unabashed relief. "Anything you can arrange will be very much appreciated. And if you would keep this just between us?"

"Miss Bryant," Harrington said.

Randall Day evidently hadn't heard her approach, and he gave a little jump, hopping like a crow. For a heavy man, he was relatively light on his feet. "Goodness, I didn't see you there."

"Mr. Day. Mr. Harrington. I hope I'm not interrupting a private—"

"Not at all," Uncle Randall said hurriedly. "Although I was just about to go in. You will excuse me?" He took two steps and turned. "Monday?"

Harrington nodded. "Monday."

"Make it Monday," she said, putting her two cents worth in for the hell of it.

When the door shut behind Uncle Randall and they were alone, she turned to Harrington. "I talked to your wife a few minutes ago."

"Did you?"

"Until she mentioned it, I hadn't realized that you and Martina were that close."

"That close, Miss Bryant?" His mouth twisted into a smile. "What are you implying?"

"Nothing. But I am curious as to what you and Martina were talking about that evening. Privately. In the library."

254

"I'd rather not say."

"Why not?"

"Why should I?" he countered. "Whatever it was, it has no bearing on the murder."

"Are you sure of that?"

"If I thought otherwise, I would have gone directly to the police. I'm an officer of the court, Miss Bryant, and for what it's worth, I would never attempt to obstruct justice."

"Should I assume that she'd consulted you regarding a legal matter?"

"Assume whatever you like."

The man had moved beyond being simply annoying and was well on his way to becoming totally infuriating. "Why did you leave a note for Martina to meet you in the Captain's Tower?"

"How did you—"

"Find out about that?" She smiled; turnabout was such fun. "I'd rather not say."

For the first time, Harrington appeared off-balance. He ran a hand through his hundred dollar haircut and pursed his lips in thought. After a minute, he asked: "What is it you're after?"

"The truth."

"Do you consider me a suspect?"

"No. Not now."

"But you did. Is it your disappointment at not being able to prove me a murderer that is driving you to destroy my marriage?"

How many times had she heard this same refrain from married men? As though it wasn't the unfaithfulness that was wrong, but only the revealing of it . . .

"If telling the truth destroys your marriage, it won't be as a result of anything I've done," she said quietly. "I have no desire to hurt your wife any more than she's already been hurt."

"It isn't what you think."

If she let him, he would dance around the issue till the cows came home. So she got straight to the point: "Were you having or had you had an affair with Martina?"

"No."

"Then what are you hiding?"

Harrington sighed. "I can see there's no reasoning with you. Let's find a place where there's a little more privacy, and we'll talk."

They settled for walking along the driveway after Sydney exchanged her heels for moccasins. The on-and-off rain was off again, but the air was fragrant with the earthy smell of wet dirt and damp grass.

To the west, a fog bank loomed, awaiting the night before moving in from the sea.

"Martina was special, the daughter I never

256

had. I loved her, but not in the way you think."

"I'm keeping an open mind."

"Please do. This past summer, she came to me, deeply troubled. It seems that during the course of some research she was conducting at the newspaper, she'd happened upon information that on several occasions over the years, I had frequented a rather exclusive club . . ."

"A club. Does this club have a name?"

"That kind of place seldom does."

She had a pretty good notion what he meant, but asked anyway: "What kind of place?"

"A place where young women made themselves available to older men."

"I see. Was her information correct?"

"Yes, unfortunately it was. I will not explain myself to you, except to say that it was in the interest of saving my marriage that I went to this club."

And if you believe that . . .

"These young women," she said, trying to ignore her cynical side, "were less demanding than a mistress would be?"

"Very perceptive of you. At any rate, Martina was quite upset and not altogether rational about it." He paused. "It was painful to me, to see the disappointment in her eyes, and hear it in her voice."

257

Sydney's sympathies remained with Martina.

"She demanded that I never go there again, and I promised that I never would."

"Did you keep your word?"

He made no attempt to hide his irritation. "Of course I did. I'm not a liar."

"Hmm." Sydney reached down, picked up a piece of wet gravel and tossed it down the road. "You said this happened during the summer. Had the subject come up again more recently?"

He inclined his head. "A month or two ago, I dropped by with some papers for Penelope to sign. We were in the living room when Martina came home. We could see that she'd been crying, but when her grandmother asked what was wrong, she just shook her head and ran from the room."

"Go on."

"I went to her bedroom—by some miracle she hadn't locked the door—and tried to get her to tell me what was bothering her."

"Did she?"

"When she wanted, Martina could be a stubborn little thing." Harrington stopped walking and turned to look back at the house, as though he expected to see her there. "She told me to leave her alone. I started to go, but first I went to pick up her jacket which had fallen to the floor, and a matchbook dropped out of the pocket."

"I take it wasn't from Disneyland," Sydney said, more to herself than to him.

If he had in fact heard her, it didn't show in his eyes, which seemed to be focused inward. "She'd gotten it from the club. There's a silhouette of a Victorian house on the cover, and nothing more."

"Did you ask her about it?"

"Yes, but she wouldn't answer. Not then."

They began walking again, this time back toward the house. "But later?"

Harrington nodded. "She came to my office the next day."

Sydney waited.

"She told me that she'd decided to do a story on the club for her senior project. Apparently she'd managed to amass a fairly significant amount of information, and all she needed was something first-hand to pull it all together."

"By first-hand, you mean—"

"She'd gone out there the day before to apply for a job."

This time it was Sydney who stopped. "A job?"

"Perhaps a third of the young women who work there are college students. It pays very well, and if you saw them, you'd never guess

259

how they earned their tuition."

"A sexual scholarship."

"More or less." He resumed walking and Sydney followed. "Anyway, while she was there, she saw something that upset her. As I said, she came home in tears."

"She didn't say what upset her?"

"Not in so many words. Whatever it was, it prompted her to abandon the idea of an exposé. She'd brought in all of her notes, and asked that I shred them."

"Which you did."

"Yes, with her watching. And that was the end of that."

Sydney wasn't as sure of that as he seemed to be. "But Tuesday . . . what did you talk about on Tuesday?"

"It was nothing really. She wanted to ask me if I'd taken that matchbook, which she thought was missing from her room. She collected them . . . almost obsessively. Between her matchbooks and Penelope's curios, they've filled a warehouse or two."

"So your reluctance to answer my questions . . ."

"I didn't want to open the proverbial can of worms. And I didn't feel that it was any of your business."

"What about the meeting at the Captain's Tower?"

He smiled sadly. "I just wanted to explain to her about Julie. That it was me Julie was angry with, and not her. I wanted to assure her that everything would be all right."

But it hadn't been.

Chapter Thirty-five

Sydney unlocked the passenger door of the Thunderbird and pushed the seat forward, but as she reached into the back for her slacks and sweater, she heard shouting behind her and froze.

"Fuck you," a young male voice shouted. "I don't need you telling me how to run my life!"

"Chad, come back here."

"Go to hell!"

Sydney turned and saw Chad Fuller trotting across the drive toward his Jeep, which was parked three cars ahead of hers. He'd unburdened himself of his funeral suit and was wearing jeans, a white t-shirt, and a Levi jacket. He still wore the paratrooper boots, the better to kick showers of gravel at anything in his way.

Looking toward the house, Sydney saw David Saxon—who should have been at the stables with Felice—turn away in a pantomime of disgust and go inside.

The door slammed behind David, and in response, Chad Fuller turned a hundred and eighty degrees to gesture obscenely. As emphatic as the expression was, it was a wonder he didn't dislocate a shoulder . . .

When he reached the Jeep he hit the hood with both fists, kicked a tire, and ran around to the driver's side. He continued to swear with great vigor and inventiveness, if slightly less volubly.

She reacted on instinct, getting in the passenger side and climbing over the console. The ignition key, thankfully, was easily identifiable, and it only took a second to start the engine.

The Jeep, which had also parallel-parked, did not observe the etiquette of un-parking, but instead rammed into the car behind it before turning left onto the manicured grounds and roaring across the yard until it was beyond the line of cars.

"That's just great." Sydney had backed up carefully until the Thunderbird's rear bumper kissed the car behind her, but since the Jeep was roaring away, she didn't have time to be as careful pulling out. She turned the wheel as far as it would go, tapped the accelerator and winced in preparation for impact.

The left front bumper missed the car ahead by the width of an extra coat of paint.

Sydney gunned the engine and felt the tires spin on the gravel. A second later the V-8 lived up to its reputation and got her out of there.

Reason told her that following a Jeep shouldn't be all that difficult, given its distinctive profile. And Cousin Chad might slow down once he was off private property; the way he drove, he probably had a glovebox full of tickets, and wouldn't want to risk another one.

At least, that was her theory.

Her theory was wrong.

Overhead, the clouds were breaking up to reveal a full moon, but there was still moisture in the air, and she had to turn on the wipers. The dirt on the windshield smeared, and in the ten seconds she fumbled to find the washer lever, she lost sight of the Jeep.

There wasn't a single set of tail lights ahead on the two-lane road.

"Damn it."

She eased off the accelerator, and looked for any sign he'd turned off, perhaps onto another private road. A mile later, when she still hadn't spotted him, she pulled onto the shoulder and came to a stop.

The Fullers, she knew, lived in Fallbrook. She'd written their street address down in her notebook, which she retrieved from under the seat. She had a Thomas Guide, and a flashlight.

She'd gotten lost in Fallbrook, once, in broad daylight. She'd had her Thomas Guide then, too.

Estimating her chances of finding the Fuller house at fifty-fifty, she glanced in the rear-view mirror to make sure it was safe and, seeing the road was empty behind her, pulled back into the lane.

A second later, headlights flashed in the mirror, but since they appeared too close to the ground to be the Jeep's, she disregarded them.

This time she did not get lost.

Long winding driveways seemed to run in the family; the Fuller house sat at least half a mile back from the road. Only the porch light shining in the darkness marked its place.

Sydney drove slowly, avoiding water-filled potholes since she couldn't tell how deep they might be. The driveway was wider than the Saxons' but there were ditches on either side.

As she neared the house, she saw that the Jeep was parked in front, along with a 4x4 pick-up with oversized tires and a light-adorned roll-bar.

"At least something's going right," she muttered.

When she was a hundred yards from the house, the front door opened. Three young men

265

came out to stand on the porch, managing to convey belligerence by their stance.

She applied the brakes and considered coming back another day.

Then she identified Chad Fuller among the three. However foul-mouthed he'd been toward cousin David, he was a member of a prominent family. This, she thought, was bravado . . . standing his ground with his parents away.

She parked and got out of the car.

"What the hell do you want?" Chad Fuller asked before she'd taken a single step. The three of them stood near the back of the car, Chad in front and the other two flanking him.

So much for the exchange of pleasantries. "I want to ask you a few questions about Martina Saxon's death."

"Yeah? You a cop?"

"I'm a private investigator—"

"Oooh," one of the others said. "Does that mean you want to investigate my privates?"

Sydney ignored him. "I've been hired by—"

"The old biddy," Chad said with obvious disgust. "I heard she was throwing money at the problem. That's what she always does."

The third member of the group snorted. "Hey, she can throw money at me anytime. I was born a problem. Ask my old man."

"If he *is* your old man. Your mama is awful

266

affectionate with that old German shepherd of yours."

"Up yours."

"Shut up, assholes," Chad said. His leadership was evidenced by the fact that they did.

"All anyone wants is to find out who killed your cousin," Sydney said. "I've been talking to everyone who was at the house that night—"

"And now you've gotten around to me." He folded his arms across his chest. "But why should I talk to you? The cops already gave me a hard time about Martina; I don't need another shit-load of misery."

Rather than argue her case, she asked, "Did you and she get along?"

"Most of the time, yeah."

"How did she seem to you that night?"

While he considered the question, he scratched and picked at a dime-sized scab on his left elbow, then tore it off. The wound bled and he wiped it on his t-shirt, leaving a bloody smear.

"About the same as usual," he said finally. "Sort of quiet, though."

"Did you see her after dinner?"

"That depends on what you mean." He examined his elbow and frowned. "I didn't talk to her, but we passed in the hall."

"Where exactly in the hall?"

"What do you mean, exactly?"

"It's a very long hall," she pointed out. "Which wing of the house were you in?"

"Near her room. She came out of her room."

"Was she alone?"

His mouth contorted into a sneer. "What do you think? The old lady is so tight-assed about what goes on under her roof, I'm surprised she lets my aunt and uncle sleep in the same bed."

"That's not what I meant." Although she did find it interesting. "When you saw her, was there anyone else in the hall?"

"Nope. Just her in her bathrobe."

"Did you see where she went?"

"One of the other bedrooms. I heard her knocking on the door when I turned the corner."

Sydney nodded, as though she'd already known this and was simply confirming her information. "Do you know whose door it was?"

"Yeah, right. A closed door is a closed door; they all look the same from the outside."

"I suppose so. After you went around the corner, did you hear voices?"

The taller of Chad's cohorts snickered. "Hell, he's on medication for that."

"Fuller," the other said, "doesn't like the rubber room."

Chad reacted so quickly that all she saw was a blur. He swung his right hand and hit the first guy hard in the throat, dropping him to his

268

knees, then rammed his still-bleeding elbow into the other one's stomach.

Then, deliberately, he raised his boot and aimed a flatfooted kick at the side of his first target's head.

Sydney took a step backward, watching him intently as he turned back to her.

"I didn't hear anything," he said through clenched teeth. "Okay?"

"Fine." Her fingers sought the recessed door handle, and found it.

A sheen of sweat made his face glisten in the yellow light from the porch, and his eyes appeared to darken as his pupils enlarged.

He's getting off on this, she thought.

Neither of his 'friends' made any move to retaliate. The one who'd been kicked in the head had flopped over onto his back and was staring glassily at the sky. The other had back-tracked to the other side of the drive.

"Shit, look what you made me do."

Blood ran down his left arm and was dripping off his fingers; the force of the blow he'd delivered had apparently torn the wound farther open.

Sydney pulled up on the handle, but as the door opened, Chad straight-armed it shut again, missing her by at best an inch.

"I don't want any trouble," she said, and thought longingly of her Smith and Wesson

269

locked in the dash. "I'll just go . . ."

"You're gonna go, all right. Son of a bitch, it won't stop." He brought his left hand to his mouth and licked blood off his fingers.

"Chad . . . I don't know what the problem is here, but this isn't going to help matters."

"Isn't going to help matters," he mimicked. "Well, isn't that a damn fucking shame."

She had no one to blame but herself for this; witnessing his temper tantrum at Villa Saxon should have given her a clue. "All I want to do is leave."

"Oh, I think you should leave," he said, and nodded vigorously, "but maybe you'd better walk."

"Then I'll walk." She backed away, one hand on the car to guide her while she kept her eyes on him. No way would she turn her back on him.

But Fuller didn't come after her. He spent a few seconds probing his bloody wound, and, when she had reached the driveway, headed for the house.

The porchlight switched off after he went inside.

Sydney walked quickly down the driveway, hampered somewhat by her skirt. The moonlight allowed her to see the potholes, but she almost lost her footing once or twice, skidding in the mud.

The sound of an engine starting caught her attention.

She glanced back over her shoulder, and saw that the 4x4's lights had come on. It lurched forward, seemed to stall, and then she heard the grinding of gears before it started down the drive.

She moved to the far edge of the road.

Whoever was driving wound it up, the transmission whining at the limits of first gear before he shifted.

Sydney took that as a sign the driver was not in the best of moods.

The pick-up raced up the center of the road. The left front tire bounced into and out of a deep hole, and the rear-end slid sickeningly as the driver overcompensated in his steering. She expected the truck to go off into the ditch, but at the last second, the driver regained the road. Then the horn began to blow, and the lights on the roll-bar flashed on, blinding her . . .

She realized, then, that the pick-up had swerved and was heading straight for her.

The choice was a simple one, and she jumped feet first into the ditch.

"This is your fault, bitch!" the driver yelled as he drove by.

The first impact of landing knocked the air

from her lungs, but then she bounced and felt a shock of pain as she continued to roll down the incline. As wet as the ground was, it hadn't softened it much, and she felt bits of gravel and rock scrape her flesh.

Then she came jarringly to a stop.

Her ears were ringing, and she felt dizzy and nauseated, so she didn't try to get up. Eyes closed, she moved her arms and legs gingerly, and was amazed that nothing appeared to be broken.

A few moments of silence and then the crickets resumed their evening serenade.

The truck, apparently, had gone.

Her moccasins had come off during her fall, but rather than waste time looking for them in the dark, she stripped off her tattered pantyhose, climbed up the side of the ditch and began walking barefoot down the drive toward the road.

Already her joints and muscles had begun to stiffen and ache. Her mother would have said she had a hitch in her getalong.

Mud had soaked her down to the skin, and she shivered, but even though she had dry clothes in the Thunderbird, there was no way she was going back to get them. Not when it was probable that Chad Fuller would be watching her from inside the house.

The police would have to handle him and her belongings. That is, if she could find a phone to call them.

Ahead, a car turned into the Fuller driveway, its headlights sweeping across the road.

Sydney stopped where she was. The body shape of the vehicle wasn't that of a truck—it was low and sleek—but she wasn't taking any chances. She stood, watching cautiously as it approached.

The car was a late model burgundy Chrysler, and the window on the passenger side lowered as it came to a stop a few feet away from her.

"Need a ride?" a male voice asked.

Sydney recognized both the car and driver then; it was her old friend from the *Union-Tribune* parking lot. Twin moons were reflected in his eyeglasses as he leaned across the seat to open the door for her.

"Get in," he said. "We've got a lot to talk about."

Chapter Thirty-six

Bespectacled, middle-aged and balding, Xavier Walker proved to be a fellow private investigator.

Sydney listened numbly as he drove her to the nearest hospital emergency room, listened and wondered at how she'd misjudged the situation.

"When she hired me—Carol Travis, that is—she told me that she and the lieutenant were only separated. And that you were the cause of it."

Sydney shook her head, but said nothing.

"She wanted me to find out whatever I could about you. Said she'd use the information to get a better settlement when she went to court."

"The divorce was final in August."

"But *I* didn't know that." He glanced sideways at her. "Someone hires you, you have to have a little faith that they're telling the truth."

"I know," she said, and sighed.

"Anyway, then a funny thing happened. She

comes to my office one afternoon to pick up some photographs of you and her ex going out to dinner—this hot material after two weeks of surveillance—and she asks me, do I know anyone who can pick a lock."

"Which you do."

"Of course I do. But we both know this isn't the kind of referral you want to give to a client, particularly a woman scorned. Agreed?"

"Agreed."

"I ask her, casual-like, why she wants a lock picked, and she gives me a big production number about how the lieutenant has this family heirloom of hers and won't give it back."

"She wanted to break into Mitch's apartment?"

"So she says. Naturally, I view this with more than a little suspicion, and I suggest to her that she consult her lawyer before she does anything rash."

"Good idea."

"Considering we're talking breaking into a cop's place, yeah, I'd say it was a damned good idea. Anyway, this pisses her off, and she storms out."

They'd reached the hospital, and Walker turned into the lot, then followed a series of red-lettered signs to Emergency.

"Now, by nature I'm a curious man, so I went to the door and watched her get in a car

275

with this guy who looks a lot like her, who I come to find out later is her brother. Are you following this?"

"It's fairly straightforward."

"So far. Then I get a call from her, maybe an hour later, and what do you know, she tells me I'm fired. I'm off the case."

"That sounds like she was pissed, all right."

"But—" he favored her with a wicked smile "—no one fires Xavier Walker. I immediately distrusted her motives, and on my free time, mind you, I decided that maybe I should see what she's up to."

"Which was?"

"Obviously harassing you."

"Obviously," she said. It was a wonder Carol Travis hadn't worn out the re-dial button on her phone.

"At first there was a lot of scurrying around but which, you should pardon the expression, signified nothing. Then I followed her brother to your office the other day and watched the idiot splatter your door with fake blood he bought at a novelty shop on Balboa."

Sydney knew the place; last Halloween she'd taken her neighbor Nicole Halpern there to buy a crystal skull for a party decoration.

Walker pulled the Chrysler into a parking space opposite the E.R. entrance.

"Which rocket scientist came up with *that*

idea, I don't know, but it was so feeble, I thought to myself, 'Xavier, why don't you see what develops before you blow the whistle on them.' "

"Although you did call me at home that night to warn me . . . that *was* you, wasn't it?"

"None other. Say, do you want me to go in and get the nurse to come out with a wheel-chair for you?"

"I can walk."

"If you're sure. Wait, let me get the door." He hustled out of the car and came around to her side before she could protest, then offered her his hand.

"Thanks."

"My pleasure." They started toward the emergency entrance. "Anyway, to make a long story short, business has been kind of slow lately, and I decided that I'd better keep an eye on you to make sure the dynamic duo didn't accidentally do some damage or — "

"Someone did break into my office," she interrupted.

"Yeah, and I chased 'em away. The brother and this sleaze jockey who had to have been an ex-con."

"It was a pro job," she noted, and then winced with each step as they went down the stairs from the parking lot to the ambulance bay.

"Take it easy." Walker put an arm around her shoulder for support, apparently oblivious to the mud on her clothes. "Yeah, the jimmy was top-notch, and I was worried there for a while that they might turn up competent or something, but then they popped your car with a baseball bat. I mean, really."

Sydney laughed at his indignation, and it made her ribs ache.

"The good news is, they saw me see them do it. And I got photographs. If you or your insurance company wants them, they're yours."

"My agent will be thrilled."

The double doors to the E.R. opened automatically before them. Inside a child was screaming but by the sound of it, more from outrage than pain.

She knew the feeling.

"You know," Walker said, "that day in the Tribune parking lot, if you had agreed to have a cup of coffee with me, I might have saved you some trouble."

"Surveillance," she said by way of explanation. It was equally true that she'd jumped to an unfounded conclusion about Walker. She'd have to fight that tendency in the future.

"Ah. And here I thought you were doing busy work like I'd been doing since Thanksgiving."

"You too?"

He nodded, and the fluorescent light from overhead shone on his bare pate. "I'm so organized it hurts . . . if I never see another index card it'll be too soon. You know, I thought about offering a two-for-one sale on skip-traces to bring some business in, but what the hell, I had more fun following you."

"I'm glad you were following me tonight." Walker smiled.

The E.R. was as busy as might be expected on a Friday evening with a full moon. Two hours passed before her name was called. Then, cleaned up and dressed in a hospital gown, she lay on a stretcher awaiting the Emergency Room doctor and reflecting on what Walker had said.

The ball was clearly in her court, and she had to decide what to do about Carol Travis. Whether to tell Mitch, or indeed anyone, about Carol's actions.

The worst that had happened was that she'd been inconvenienced and annoyed. There was the expense of replacing the Mustang's window and renting a car, but maybe the best thing for everyone would be for her to pay for it herself.

The phone calls would have to stop, but she thought a call of her own might accomplish that.

She didn't want to cause trouble for Carol Travis, partly because she still felt a sense of guilt over the brief affair she and Mitch had had three years ago. She hadn't known he was married when the affair started, but when she found out—to her shame—it took her several months to end it.

But the fact was that she hadn't resumed dating him until after his divorce was granted and she'd seen the final decree with her own eyes. This time, she hadn't done anything that felt wrong to her.

This time, things were different.

The doctor cleaned up her abrasions, wrapped her left knee in an elastic bandage, gave her six Tylenol with codeine and a prescription for more, and then told her she could go home. The nurse supplied a pair of surgical greens for her to wear since her dress had been ruined.

"Oh, and Miss Bryant," the nurse said, and gave her a lucky-you grin. "Your ride is here."

Sydney shook her head at that. Xavier Walker was a nice enough man, but nothing to get excited over.

When she finished dressing, though, and pulled back the curtain, Mitch was the one waiting.

With her in over-sized greens and disposable paper booties, and him in a light gray Italian suit, black shirt and gray tie, they drew more than a few curious stares on their way out.

Chapter Thirty-seven

". . . but when they got there," Mitch said, "Fuller had gone."

That didn't surprise her; Chad Fuller would have to know that chasing her off wouldn't be the end of it. But she said, "I don't think he was driving the truck that forced me off the road."

In the faint light from the dashboard, Mitch's expression looked grim. "We'll find the others, take my word for it."

"Did you recover—"

"The T-Bird? Yes; I had them tow it to your apartment, but . . ."

She glanced at him again. "But what?"

"The news isn't good, Cochise. Someone had evidently rifled through your purse. Your driver's license was on the ground outside the car. He— or they—wanted to know where you live."

"They took my keys?"

"Oddly enough, they didn't; the keys were still

in the ignition. I guess using a key to break in would be too civilized for them."

"Mitch, are you telling me they broke into my apartment?"

"Broke in through your bedroom window, by the looks of it." He reached over, took her hand, and squeezed it. "I'm sorry, kid."

"Sweet Jesus. How much damage did they do?"

"Oh, the rough equivalent of what a rhinoceros hyped on speed might do."

Sydney felt sick to her stomach. "They trashed the place?"

"Trashed it royally," he confirmed. "Judging by the amount of damage, we think there were at least two of them, but it could have been just one extremely angry little mother-fucker."

"Wonderful." She rubbed at her temple, which had begun to throb, and then had a thought that made it worse. "Mitch . . . was the glovebox broken into?"

Mitch frowned. "The what?"

"In the car. My gun was locked in the glovebox."

"No one said anything about it. I'll call in and have someone look. I have an officer assigned to your apartment to keep an eye out."

"But that's where we're going now, isn't it? My apartment?"

"Not on your life." He glanced in the rearview mirror before changing lanes. "You're coming home with me tonight, Sydney."

"What? I —"

"Don't argue. Your apartment is uninhabitable. And even if it wasn't, I wouldn't want you staying there . . . your visitors might take in their heads to pay another unannounced call."

"Still, do you think it's a good idea?"

"Why not? I can sleep on the couch and you can have the bed. In the morning, I'll deliver you to your doorstep, and you can take it from there."

"But —"

"But nothing. Besides, I have a built-in whirlpool at my place . . ."

The whirlpool did indeed sound great, and as sore as she felt now, she knew it would only get worse.

"Okay then," she said. "All I can say is, it's a good thing Xavier Walker isn't around to see this."

Mitch's bathroom was nothing less than a work of art.

As spacious as most master bedrooms, it had a separate shower and raised black marble bathtub, two sinks in an eight-foot long vanity backed by a tinted mirror, and a skylight which easily took up half of the sloped ceiling. A

284

score of lush green hanging plants brought the outdoors in . . . and classical music played soothingly over hidden speakers.

Mitch turned the water on to fill the tub and then opened a cabinet door she would never have known was there to get fresh towels. When he turned to look at her, she could only smile.

"I'll see what I can find for you to sleep in," he said.

"The tub'll do."

Mitch laughed. "I was thinking more along the lines of a t-shirt."

"Whatever." She sat down on the side of the tub and examined the whirlpool controls. "I hadn't realized the city paid its lieutenants so well."

He came to stand beside her, then stroked her face with the back of his hand. "It's a matter of priorities. I know what—and who—is important to me."

Sydney switched on the jets and in a matter of seconds, the steaming water began to froth. "I hope you've saved enough to afford a tow-truck, because it's going to take one to get me out of here."

The whirlpool far exceeded her expectations; eight jets of aerated water massaged her aching muscles from virtually every angle.

She rested her head against the back of the tub — which had a built-in cushion — and closed her eyes. Moving her bruised and sprained left knee in front of one of the water jets, she luxuriated in the cessation of pain.

A tow-truck wouldn't do, she thought. It would take at least an act of Congress.

The bathroom door opened and Mitch came in. Sydney glanced down to see what might be showing, but the churning water offered excellent camouflage.

"I brought you a drink," he said, putting the glass down near the head of the tub. He sat down at the opposite end, facing her, and lifted his own glass in a toast. "To hydrotherapy."

She reached for her glass and raised it. "To the end of an incredibly long day."

"Almost the end," he said, watching her as she took a sip of her drink. "I talked to the officer standing watch at your apartment. He went out to check on your gun, and it's still there."

"Thank heaven."

"Not —" Mitch shook his head "— that those miscreants couldn't lay their hands on something more lethal at any time of the day or night."

"Granted, but it won't be *my* gun."

"No." He finished his drink and reached around to put the empty glass on the vanity. "So . . . where does all of this leave you?"

"The case, you mean?"

"The case. Is Chad Fuller moving up on your hit parade?"

"Well, he's certainly moved from the B list to the A list."

"Oh, *now* you've got an A and B list."

She made a minor adjustment in her position so that the whirlpool jet was directed at her left kneecap. Her right knee emerged from the water. "I always had two lists, but I didn't want to complicate matters."

"You thought I couldn't keep them straight in my head?" He trailed his fingers in the water, then began to stroke the inside of her right knee.

Sydney raised her eyebrows at him. "What are you doing?"

"Don't change the subject. Didn't you think I could remember which of your suspects were prime and which were secondary?"

"To be honest, I wasn't thinking about it one way or the other."

"No?" He moved his hand down the back of her calf, massaging gently.

"No. You aren't planning on getting in this tub with me, are you?"

"I wasn't planning on it, but if you insist . . ."

"Hmm." He was rubbing her ankle now, and if he didn't stop in the next thirty minutes or so, she'd have to move her leg. "I don't think

287

your mind is on the case."

"Sure it is. What were you saying about Fuller making the A list?"

"Just that he did. He leap-frogged right over Owen and Uncle Randall. B listers."

"And the housekeeper? See, I was listening."

"Edith's off entirely. And, darn it, so is Boyd Harrington."

"Who does that leave?" He used his thumb to knead the arch of her foot. "Felice, who you don't like."

"Don't like —" she closed her eyes "— and haven't talked to."

"There's always tomorrow."

"Right, tomorrow."

"Only why would this Felice want to kill her future sister-in-law? And in such a brutal way?"

Her eyelids were heavy, but she managed to open them half-way. "I don't know, but why would Chad kill his cousin?"

"A sudden fit of rage."

She thought of the instantaneous change that had come over Fuller and the violence of his response to his friends' innocent — if mean-spirited — comments. His reaction had been way out of line with the provocation.

"Except . . . except . . ." She blinked; she'd forgotten the point she intended to make.

"I think you're done for the night." He got up, reached for a towel, and then held it up for her to wrap herself in. "Bedtime."

"Kindly avert your eyes," she said.

He complied, staring up at the skylight as she got to her feet and pulled the towel around her.

Only his arms went around her as well.

"I'm wet," she protested.

Mitch didn't seem to mind. He lifted her out of the water and carried her, dripping, into the bedroom.

Standing by the bed, with his arms holding her tight to him, Sydney felt the heat between them reach a critical phase, near the flashpoint. She ran her hands across his back and shoulders before what remained of her willpower asserted itself and she pulled away.

"I can't," she said, still breathless from his kisses. "I ache all over from falling in that ditch."

"I ache all over, too."

She brushed her hair back from her face. "Mitch, you know I want to. I've wanted to for a long time, but I can't. Not tonight."

His eyes revealed both resignation and determination. "I'm not going to give up, Sydney. If not tonight, then some other night."

Vivid memories of the last time they'd been together sent a tingle of anticipation up her spine and made her shiver. Rather than give him the wrong idea—or the right idea—she backed away.

289

"I have something for you," he said, and smiled.

The box he placed before her on the bed was black velvet, and even before she picked it up, she knew what was inside.

A diamond ring, a full carat, beautifully faceted in its gold setting. The slightest movement displayed the white-silver fire within the stone.

"Mitch," she said, and then bit her lip.

"I bought it a couple of months ago." He removed the ring from the velvet box and took her hand. "I've been carrying it around with me ever since, waiting for the right time."

Sydney laughed quietly. "And this is it? Here I am, black and blue, with bruises on my bruises . . ."

"Who knows? Maybe you hit your head and it knocked you silly enough to say yes."

"That would be diminished capacity."

"I'll take you anyway I can get you." He slipped the ring on her finger. "Will you marry me, Sydney?"

Chapter Thirty-eight

Saturday

In the morning, Sydney surveyed the damage to her apartment as dispassionately as she could, trying to assess her losses on a financial rather than emotional basis. She didn't quite succeed; after twenty minutes of wandering back and forth through the rooms, looking at slashed cushions, torn drapes, broken mirrors, and shattered glassware, she was shaking from a sense of violation.

The apartment manager had arranged for the bedroom window to be replaced, and for her locks to be re-keyed. He handed her a card from a specialized cleaning service, which would be able to restore the apartment to some semblance of order, he said, "In a day or two."

After calling the cleaning service, she changed into jeans and her purple and gold Laker sweatshirt. She dug through clothing and other items that had been dumped out of her dresser drawers, and found the holster she'd had made so that she could wear the Smith and Wesson comfortably at the small of her back.

Then she headed for the sheriff's sub-station.

"Sydney Bryant," the desk officer said, and began to dig through his out-basket. "Right. Lieutenant Grant did leave an envelope for you."

Sydney shifted her weight onto her good leg— this morning her left knee was badly swollen— and watched patiently as he searched, although she could see that there was only one envelope of a size to contain the reports Grant had promised her.

"Here you go." He smiled as he handed the envelope to her. "Laker fan?"

"Born and bred. Thank the lieutenant for me, would you?"

"Sure thing."

Eager to review the material Grant had given her, she opened the envelope as soon as she got in the car. She'd just removed its contents when someone tapped on the passenger window.

"Shit, Kevin," she said after lowering the window. "You have the worst timing."

"Count on it." He unlocked the door and got

in the car. "But speaking of timing, I hear your case is breaking."

"It is? That's news to me."

"Always the last to know, eh? They told us at this morning's briefing that they were, and I quote, going to effectuate an arrest, unquote."

"Who are they arresting?"

"Chad Fuller. The arrest warrant was signed early this morning, but the word is he's been the primary suspect since day one."

Sydney frowned. That explained Dwight Grant's sudden willingness to share information with her; he'd made his case, and probably figured that they'd have Fuller in custody before she read a single report.

No wonder the smile when she'd asked for the blood analysis results. No wonder his plea of "previous engagements" when she'd requested that she have access to the material yesterday afternoon.

As a prince, Grant made a great frog.

She'd have to remember to thank him later. But right now she had other concerns. "What have they got on him, do you know?"

"A lot of odds and ends. His fingerprints were found in the vicinity of the victim's room—"

"What about *in* the room?"

"Not as far as I know."

"Sounds circumstantial to me. I mean, he ad-

293

mitted to being in the hallway on Tuesday night, and no doubt had been there before."

"Hey, I agree. Perry Mason would have a field day with the prints."

"What else do they have?"

"Mainly, opportunity—"

"An opportunity shared by twelve other people, Kevin," she pointed out.

"And a history of violent behavior. He's got a nice little pedigree in aggravated assault."

"Oh."

"But I shouldn't have to tell you that; I heard you got a taste of his temper."

"Word travels fast," she said, and winced. The Smith and Wesson was pressed against a tender spot on her back, and she removed it from the holster, then laid it gently on the console.

Kevin whistled. "You're carrying?"

"Don't worry, I have a permit."

"I'm not worried, but—" he picked up the .38 and put it inside the console "—if someone walks by and sees this little hummer, they'll roust you first and ask questions later."

"Thanks . . . I guess I'm not thinking straight yet this morning." All she needed was for some hulking deputy to pull her from the car and throw her to the ground with his knee in her back. She'd have to file for disability . . . or worse.

"Anyway, Mr. Chad 'I Like to Kick Ass'

Fuller will soon be in the loving comfort of the county's arms. And who knows who else's?" Kevin grinned and scratched his nose. "And you can collect your fee."

"Not so fast. What about the blood?"

"Whose blood?"

"Martina Saxon's blood. You stab someone in the back seven times and you're going to get blood on you. Were there bloodstains on Fuller's clothes?"

Kevin held his hands up in mock surrender. "I'm not the one to ask."

"Hold the phone," Sydney said, and began paging through the reports Grant had released to her, albeit after the fact. She found a group of physical evidence reports stapled together and skimmed over them.

"Where'd you get those?" Kevin asked.

"From my fairy godmother. Look at this, Kevin . . . no bloodstains were found on Chad Fuller's or anyone else's clothes."

"Maybe Fuller wrapped himself in Saran Wrap before he killed her —"

"That doesn't sound opportunistic to me."

"Hey, I shouldn't be facetious and I'll admit I don't have all the facts, but I think the case is solid, okay? And remember, the judge who signed the warrant found sufficient cause for arrest."

"There's still something about all of this that bothers me."

"But," he said, *"but* . . . if you were to line up everyone who was there that night, which one out of all of them best fits the part?"

"Chad Fuller," she admitted.

"And you know he's into that pseudo-commando type shit—"

"I didn't know." There were the paratrooper boots, but she knew a bank vice-president who swore they were the only boots worth the name . . .

"Well, he is. Maybe he's learned a way to kill someone at close range without spilling a lot of blood."

"I suppose."

"What I'm trying to say is that only in one case in a million is every question answered. We may never know why there wasn't blood on Fuller's clothes."

"Or anyone else's," she mused.

Before heading out to Villa Saxon, she read every report and every statement, down to the last crossed T, dotted i and period.

It gave her a lot to think about as she drove.

Chapter Thirty-nine

At the crest of the hill, where Villa Saxon first came into view, Sydney eased the Thunderbird to a stop.

The estate really was breath-taking, classically elegant and reminiscent, she thought, of an earlier time. From this vantage point, it seemed to offer an idyllic existence, an escape from a less civilized world.

The only flaw she could see were the tire tracks Chad Fuller had left behind after driving over the manicured lawn. But already there was a groundskeeper tending to that, and in a few days or a week there'd be no visible sign of damage to the grounds.

Other scars ran deeper.

Miss Penelope was just leaving as Sydney arrived. In contrast to yesterday's mourning black, the matriarch was dressed in a crisp linen suit the color of daffodils. Her wide-brimmed hat cast her face in shadow, but there was nothing dark about her smile.

"Sydney," Miss Penelope said, and nestled Sydney's hand between hers. "Have you heard? The police discovered who killed Martina."

"Yes, I know."

"I am devastated, of course, for Chad's family—Boyd is this very minute trying to locate them in Europe—but they really should have done something about the boy ten years ago."

"I wasn't aware that the problem was that longstanding." She walked slowly with Miss Penelope toward the limousine.

"Perhaps longer. I know Amanda tried to tell her sister that the child needed help, and even offered to pay for a psychiatrist, but Susannah Fuller would have none of it."

"That seems curious."

"Doesn't it? If you want my opinion, the woman simply didn't want to be bothered. She hadn't married as well as Amanda, and I've often thought all the gadding about she does is her way of denying her circumstances."

"Which are?" Sydney prompted.

Miss Penelope dabbed at her face with a handkerchief she'd had tucked in her sleeve. "All of the Fullers are on the fringe. The family was a good one, two generations ago, but since then they've been more concerned with appearances than actuality."

298

"Interesting," she said, thinking that Chad had learned that lesson well, only he'd chosen the other extreme by flaunting his bad-boy image.

"Heaven knows what lengths Susannah will have to go to as a way of denying what her son has done."

If he'd done anything at all.

"I realize I should have told you about Chad's little difficulty . . ."

"It might have helped."

". . . but I didn't want to bias you against the poor boy, even though he's not a blood relation."

Hearing beyond the words, Sydney detected Miss Penelope's relief at that; how much worse for the family if Martina had been murdered by one of *them*. How convenient to find a killer related only by marriage.

The chauffeur held the door open for Miss Penelope, ready to assist her in, but even as she accepted his steadying hand she hesitated and turned to Sydney with a frown.

"I do wonder why he did it, though."

Blood will tell, Sydney thought, but said nothing.

Edith Armstrong answered the door with her usual severe manner. "Oh, it's you."

Sydney smiled. "Nice to see you too, Edith. May I come in?"

The housekeeper stood aside. "I won't be answering any more questions, I'll have you know. I've already told you more than I intended."

"Well, I—"

"If you want to know any more from me, you'll have to read it in my book."

"No questions, except . . . is Felice here?"

"That one." Edith shut the door. "She's out by the pool, sunning herself."

"On an overcast day?"

The housekeeper smiled grimly. "There are sunlamps mounted above the pool. No cloudy sky would dare interfere with her plans."

"I suppose not. Now if you'll excuse me, I'd like to have a word with her," Sydney said, heading for the courtyard.

But Edith hadn't finished. "I've caught her out there many a time sunbathing in the nude, so consider yourself forewarned."

"Thank you, Edith."

The housekeeper's voice followed her as she turned the corner: "Doesn't give a thought that David and Owen will be finishing their tennis match soon and traipsing through, and there she'll be, pretty as you please."

Chapter Forty

Arranged fetchingly on a reclining lounge chair as she basked under a row of sunlamps, Felice McDaniel narrowly avoided nudity, compliments of a knit string bikini which went a long way to reveal her assets.

Walking to that side of the pool, Sydney observed a sudden stillness which told her that, behind the cover of dark glasses, Felice was watching her.

"Good morning," she said. "Mind if I sit down and share your sun?"

Felice laughed unconvincingly. "Be my guest."

Sydney pulled up a chair and sat, stretching out her left leg so her knee wouldn't stiffen. "I assume you've heard about Chad."

With a slight nod, Felice said, "David's grandmother announced it at breakfast this morning. That detective, the big one—"

"Dwight Grant?"

"Yes, Grant. He called her as a courtesy to inform her that an arrest was forthcoming."

"Nice of him." Sydney managed to keep the sarcasm out of her voice.

"We thought so. Of course, Amanda was understandably disturbed by the news, but to the rest of us, the news came as quite a relief."

"I can imagine," she said, and thought, to some more than others.

"Amanda wanted to rush down to the jail and wait for Chad to be brought in, to ask him why . . ."

"Did she go?"

Felice shook her head. "Jared felt that it would be too much for her, so soon after the funeral. He took her to the beach house for the week-end instead."

The rich always have options, Sydney thought, and then felt guilty, because of all of the Saxons, she had the most empathy for Amanda.

"Besides," Felice continued, reaching for a glass of orange juice on the small table next to the lounge, "it may be days before they find Chad."

Considering how short the distance was to the Mexican border, Sydney thought it could take longer, and might even be more of an 'if' than a 'when.'

"How's the rest of the family taking the news?"

Felice sipped her orange juice before replying. "I'm probably not the one you should ask. I'm

302

still an outsider, and will be until the wedding."

"When were you and David planning to get married?"

"The tenth of January."

"That soon?"

"It feels more like it's an eternity from now; the day can't come soon enough to suit me."

"You won't postpone it. I mean —"

"I know exactly what you mean." Felice's smile had an edge to it. She took off her sunglasses and began to polish them with the corner of her towel. "But life goes on. It makes no sense to postpone getting on with our future . . . and if not January, when?"

Sydney returned an equivalent smile. Felice's response seemed practiced to her, and she decided that it was time to redirect the conversation. "How did you and David happen to meet?"

"Oh." Felice's green cat's eyes revealed her surprise at the question, but she answered, if vaguely. "At a party at a friend's house."

"His friend or yours? Or was this a mutual friend?"

"Jack is an old friend of David's from his prep school days, but I really don't see that it matters one way or another."

"You never know," Sydney said. "How did you come to be at the party?"

The glasses went back on, shielding her expression. "I can't honestly recall."

303

"Really?" she asked, and thought, *Or prefer not to say?*

"Really."

"That's interesting, because I think I'd remember each second and every detail of the first time I met the man of my dreams."

"Not all of us are romantics," Felice said.

Or maybe, Sydney thought, David wasn't what Felice dreamed about. "I take it, then, that it wasn't love at first sight?"

"I'm not sure there is such a thing." Felice ran a hand over her flat belly, then tugged ineffectually at her bikini. "But I grew to love him."

"And now," she said wonderingly, "you can hardly wait to marry him."

"Yes."

"Will your family be flying out for the wedding?"

The tip of her tongue licked at her full upper lip for perhaps ten seconds before she answered. "My mother is an invalid, and my father seldom leaves her side. No, they won't be attending."

"No brothers or sisters?"

"I'm an only child."

"Aunts? Uncles? Cousins?"

"None living."

"That's a shame. It's odd, but somehow I got the impression that you came from a larger family . . . one of those grand old Southern dynasties with an eccentric for each limb of the family tree."

Felice shrugged her slender shoulders. "Your impression was wrong."

"I imagine being thrust into an extended family like David's must have taken some getting used to."

"I adapt quickly."

"Evidently. Still, how sad for your parents, that they won't be at their only child's wedding."

"Yes, isn't it?"

"Had you thought of having the wedding at your parents' house?"

"That simply isn't possible. My mother and father are quite elderly, besides my mother's infirmity. The excitement would be .too much for them."

"You could have a simple ceremony at their home, and a second formal service here—"

"I'm flattered by your interest," Felice interrupted, her tone suggesting otherwise, "but David and I both feel we've made the right decision."

"Well, I'm sure you know what's best . . ."

"I think so."

Sydney regarded her thoughtfully for a moment, then nodded. "Who is going to be your maid of honor now that Martina is dead?"

Felice started visibly at the mention of Martina's name, and Sydney felt a sense of satisfaction in that; she hadn't seen the question coming.

"I won't have a maid of honor," she said.

"There isn't anyone who could take Martina's place?" Sydney noted that Felice had begun rubbing her thumb and forefinger together, and wondered whether it was a conscious or subconscious act.

"Of course not."

"I mean in the wedding party."

"I know what you meant," Felice snapped. "I know very well what you—"

"A close friend of yours, someone you worked with at the club?"

"I don't know what you're talking about." Any pretense of cordiality was gone. "What club?"

"Felice," Sydney said, "didn't Martina come to you and tell you she knew about the club?"

Felice said nothing.

"Didn't she say to you that she had to tell David what she'd found out?"

Silence.

"Weren't you afraid that if she told him, he'd call your engagement off?"

Felice reached over for her orange juice and took a sip. Her hand was steady, her gaze cool.

"Didn't you kill Martina to keep that secret?"

A smile played at one corner of her mouth. "Chad Fuller killed Martina."

"I don't think he did." Sydney frowned, troubled by the lack of a response. "I think you killed her. I think you had too much to lose."

"And how did I do it?"

The question was posed in such a measured manner that Sydney had a moment of doubt. She pushed it aside. "On Tuesday night, you asked Martina to come to your room on some pretext. Maybe you said you could explain."

"How devious of me."

"Chad saw Martina in the hallway and heard her knocking on a door—"

"My door?" Felice laughed softly. "I don't think it was my door."

"It had to have been. You talked and probably argued, and she went to leave, but you blocked her way and she ran out into the courtyard."

"Other rooms open on the courtyard," she said, "from all sides."

"And you followed her, Felice. You followed her and stabbed her repeatedly, watched her body fall in the water, and knew she was dying."

Felice removed her sunglasses; there was amusement in her eyes. "This is fascinating, in a repulsive kind of way, but I'm afraid it's all in your mind."

"Is it? David came to your door to talk to you, but you wouldn't let him in."

"I wasn't dressed. I was about to step into the shower."

"A curious display of modesty, considering that you sunbathe in the nude—"

307

"When no one's around."

Sydney shook her head. "I've heard otherwise."

"An insignificant point, but one which I'll concede, since it has nothing to do with anything."

"Doesn't it?"

Felice gave an exaggerated sigh. "Do you think I was standing behind that closed door, whispering sweet nothings to my fiance with his sister's blood dripping from my hands? Do you?"

This time Sydney remained silent.

"And did I tear up the carpet where the blood dripped and re-paint the door where I touched it? Did I burn my bloodstained clothes in the sink and flush the ashes down the toilet?"

"You didn't have to."

Felice ignored her. "And if I didn't do all of that, couldn't have *done* all of that, why didn't the police find a spot of blood in my room?"

"It's funny you should mention that," Sydney said evenly. "The lack of bloodstains bothered me for the longest time. Stabbing is a messy way to kill someone. When the knife is pulled out, some of the blood on the blade is flung off."

Those feline eyes narrowed.

"The blood splatters onto whoever is doing the stabbing and beyond them. In an ordinary room, it isn't unusual for there to be blood on

308

the ceiling . . ."

"Not a spot," Felice repeated. "They didn't find a single drop of blood in my room."

Sydney glanced up. "Of course, in this case, the ceiling is too high for a spray of blood to reach, but the murder was done at close quarters, and must have gotten messy indeed."

"Ask Chad about that."

"I read all of the police reports earlier this morning, and I know that they didn't find any blood on his clothing, except for one miniscule smear on his left boot."

"So he cleaned up somewhere. He doesn't live here, remember. He changed and buried the clothes he was wearing under an avocado tree."

"You're the one who cleaned up, Felice. Only you didn't have to rip up bloodstained carpet and burn your clothes, because you were nude when you killed Martina."

Felice took a sudden intake of breath.

"It's the only solution that makes any sense. The reason you didn't open the door for David was that Martina was in your room at that moment."

"That is . . . totally a figment of your imagination. Your fevered imagination."

"Is it? Chad said she was in her bathrobe when he saw her, but her body was recovered in only the slip she was wearing underneath. It doesn't take a fevered imagination to conceive of you grabbing at her, her robe slipping off in your hand."

"You are certifiable, Miss Bryant."

"You dropped your own robe to the floor as well, and went after her—"

"With a knife I just happened to have with me?" Felice laughed derisively. "A rather primitive item for a bridal trousseau."

"An essential item," Sydney countered. "Without it, there might not have been a wedding."

"This is getting very tiresome, so why don't you—how do they say it in Hollywood?—cut to the chase."

"You caught up to her and stabbed her—"

"Yes, yes, I know that part. Go on."

"And then you dove into the pool with her body." Sydney felt her heartbeat quicken, seeing an almost animal keenness in Felice's green eyes. "She may not have been dead yet, but that didn't matter. You swam around long enough to rinse Martina's blood from your bare skin."

"No."

"Yes. Then you got out and went back to your shower, which probably had been running all the while, so that if David came back, he wouldn't wonder why you weren't answering the door."

"No."

"You and David were the last to leave the house that night."

"No, that can't be—"

"I saw you leave, and at first I thought that

wearing your hair slicked back was merely a fashion choice, but now I know you were in such a hurry to be gone that you couldn't take the time to blow-dry your hair."

Felice covered her mouth with her hand, which now was shaking.

"Killing Martina did upset your schedule, didn't it? A minor inconvenience, I suppose."

"You can't prove any of it."

"Now that they'll know what to look for . . . chlorine in your carpet instead of blood . . . Martina's robe hung up in your closet . . . and a motive in her knowledge of your association with the club."

Felice actually laughed. "What to look for, my ass. The chlorine? I think they'd find that in all of the rooms facing the courtyard. And why shouldn't Martina have loaned me a robe?"

"Chad may be able to identify it."

"There's an even chance he won't," she retorted, lifting her chin. "And as for a motive . . . I'm not sure where you came up with the idea, but I've never been to this *club* you keep talking about, although I'm going to guess that it's an unsavory place."

Sydney hesitated, momentarily uncertain. There hadn't been time to check out the particulars of the club, but in the scenario she'd developed, Martina had somehow stumbled onto the fact that Felice had once worked there.

Quite possibly there were photographs of the

311

"girls" in the manager's office or perhaps a Rolodex with names and numbers. While waiting
for her interview, Martina would have done a
little investigating of her own . . . and could
have come across indisputable evidence that her
future sister-in-law wasn't what she claimed to
be.

Naturally, Martina had been upset—

*There could be any number of things in a
place like that which might have upset Martina
. . . none of them having to do with Felice Mc-
Daniel.*

"Without the club," Felice said smugly, "your
theory falls completely apart."

Not completely, Sydney thought, but close.
Had she blown it that badly?

"This has been amusing, Miss Bryant, but I
don't think we have anything else to discuss."
She swung her legs off the lounge and began to
collect her belongings.

If she went to Dwight Grant with her suspicions, would he act on them? Admittedly, the
police could point to no reason for Chad Fuller
to have killed his cousin, but his history of violence substituted for motive.

History, Sydney thought, and blinked. "What
about genealogy?"

Felice McDaniel froze.

"Martina had ordered a book on genealogy,
and she also had access to the newspaper's files.
What was she looking for, do you think?"

A little of the color drained from her face.

"This is a family that puts great faith in bloodlines." She spoke quietly. "Miss Penelope would never approve of her eldest grandson marrying beneath him."

Felice met her eyes and Sydney saw the truth in them.

"There'll be records at the newspaper, which files she took out and when."

"No." The word was whispered.

"My God, Felice," a male voice said.

Sydney turned and saw David Saxon standing across the courtyard with brother Owen behind him. How long they'd been there she didn't know, but David's face was ashen, his eyes wide with shock.

"David, it isn't what you think . . ."

"Martina told me she was going to do a family history for us as a wedding present, and I told you. Did you kill my sister?"

Felice didn't answer.

Epilogue

January 10th

Sydney sat at her desk, writing checks to pay Bryant Investigation's bills. Every time she dated a check, she found herself frowning.

Today would have been David Saxon and Felice McDaniel's wedding day.

David Saxon had embarked on a month-long sojourn to the south of France, accompanied by Randall Day, who swore that he would show his grand-nephew the time of his life.

Felice McDaniel, on the other hand, was looking at spending a lifetime behind bars, provided that the district attorney didn't make this a death penalty case.

Felice's elderly parents turned out to be her grandparents, who'd raised her after her mother and stepfather were killed in a fire of suspicious origin. Felice had been ten years old when they died.

No one knew who her natural father was, but

the rumor in the small town she'd grown up in was that her birth was the result of an incestuous union. Opinion was divided fifty-fifty as to whether it was old Calvin McDaniel who'd gotten to his daughter and sired his granddaughter, or one of the dozens of McDaniel cousins, known far and wide to be a randy bunch.

The family history Felice had related to David was of gentility and grace, of balmy Southern nights on the veranda, and of aristocratic bloodlines that went back as far as the Civil War.

David had been so smitten, he'd taken her word as gospel and never thought to question why she'd never taken him home to meet her parents.

Felice, the chameleon, adapted to the trappings of wealth without the slightest difficulty. Beautiful and stylish, everyone agreed she would be an elegant addition to the family.

If it had crossed anyone's mind that she wasn't all that she appeared to be, those doubts had gone unspoken.

For her part, Felice was staying silent. Her court-appointed attorney routinely refused requests for interviews with the young woman the press was ghoulishly calling the Blood Bride.

The Sheriff's Department had located Chad Fuller roughly at the same time Dwight Grant had arrived at Villa Saxon to take Felice into custody. Because of an unspecified glitch in communications, Fuller was subdued rather forcefully, but not before he broke a deputy's arm.

Charges were pending on both sides: Fuller having filed a civil lawsuit charging unlawful arrest using undue force, and the county countering with a criminal count of assaulting a law officer.

Boyd Harrington was Fuller's attorney of record in the civil case, and his influence helped retain one of the city's best defense lawyers for the criminal case. Miss Penelope was paying all legal costs.

Amanda Saxon had disappeared from the social scene.

Jared Saxon somehow convinced Owen to work for one of the family's businesses, where Owen was said to have perfected the four-hour lunch.

Victor was working around the clock, as usual, although he avoided stories relating to any aspect of the Blood Bride case. They'd had lunch after the first of the year, and she had been relieved to find that he was almost his obnoxious old self.

Life went on.

Sydney licked the last envelope and surveyed the stack of bills. Strange that it seemed that

316

the less she spent, the more she owed. Even with Miss Penelope's generous compensation, her bottom line for last year showed a net loss from the year before.

Xavier Walker had proposed a solution to that, suggesting that they merge their operations.

"Think of it: we can split the overhead while moving up to better offices. We'll eliminate duplication—I have a photocopier, you have a photocopier, I have a darkroom, you have a darkroom—and save hand over fist."

"I don't know, Xavier."

"I can't afford to pay a full-time secretary, and neither can you, but if we throw in together, we can swing it. Think of it: someone else to do your filing, someone else to transcribe your notes . . ."

"It does sound great," she'd said.

"And there'll be two of us to divide the workload. I mean, we can spell each other on those eighteen hour surveillances, and don't you know, sometimes two heads are plain better than one."

"But—"

"How does this sound, Bryant and Walker Investigations Incorporated?"

"You've been at this longer than I have," she pointed out. "Shouldn't it be Walker and Bryant?"

"I'm not a man with ego," Xavier Walker

317

said, and laughed. "Alphabetically, it makes more sense the other way. And pardon me if I sound like a sexist pig, but ladies first."

"But do we really need to incorporate?"

"It's the only way. Come on, what do you say? We'd be a great team . . . with a secretary."

"It does sound tempting," she'd admitted. "But give me till the end of the week to think it over."

"Sure enough, partner."

The end of the week was today. The more she thought about a partnership, the more she liked the idea. If nothing else, during the slow times, they could throw paper airplanes at each other . . .

Sydney glanced at her watch and carried the stack of envelopes to the door. The mail was late again today, but this time it had saved her a trip to the post office to mail the bills off.

Right now she needed to drive over to the Clairemont Mesa to keep the appointment she'd made to have the cellular phone her mother had given her for Christmas installed in the Mustang.

At last, a cellular phone!

Mom was expecting her to dinner later this evening, and of course she'd want to see her gift put to good use.

"But don't you dare put an answering machine on the phone in your car," her mother had said.

And then there was Mitch. He'd called her three times today, asking what he should wear to dinner at her mother's. The man was a nervous wreck.

Sydney glanced down at the ring on the third finger of her left hand.

And smiled.